UNHOLY CRAVING

SINFUL NATURES 1

LYNN BURKE

UNHOLY CRAVING

As a newly appointed youth pastor, I blindly walk by faith, stumbling without the promised light down God's chosen path.

Until a young man resurrects the sinful nature I've rejected in my strive for purity.

Isaac Van Dusen, my pastor's son.

He's troubled. Rebellious. Off limits to my lonely heart, yet gives me breath when I feel I'm drowning and in need of a savior.

Isaac's hunger for sin rivals mine, the kind that consumes.

Burns like fire and brimstone.

I'm determined to stay in a constant state of prayer, begging for delivery from temptation—all while dreaming of being on my knees for entirely different reasons.

I want to submit to the unholy craving between

us and worship the young man entrusted to my spiritual care.

But acting on the lusts of the flesh ensures our fall from grace, and I can't allow him to be the second one to pay the price for my sins.

Even if it means living a lie for eternity.

1

———

MALACHI

I sat outside Elkins Bible Church, my hands still gripping my old truck's steering wheel. The rust bucket had gotten me and all my meager belongings from the outskirts of Frederick, Maryland to the deep woods of northern Pennsylvania without breaking down, surprisingly.

Dad's '48 Chevy truck had outlived him by six months, and while it was a piece of junk, I couldn't bear to part with the one thing we'd had together outside of church when I was younger. His garage, his baby, grease and laughter.

Inhaling deeply, I forced my hands to move— wiping my damp palms on my dress pants and turning off the key to cut the rumbling engine.

I had promised myself a new beginning, one in the small community of Elkins as the new youth pastor for a tiny group of fifteen teens. Quiet, where no angst or strife would riddle my hollowed-out heart.

Lord, help me.

That prayer lingering in my head, I opened the truck's squeaky door to the spring's cool breeze. Sunlight glinted off the side mirror, blinding me for a brief moment as the pebbled parking lot crunched beneath my dress shoes. When my vision cleared, a forty-something man stood on the church's small porch, smiling my way.

We hadn't met in person, but I recognized him from my virtual interview a few weeks earlier.

"Malachi?" he called, his light steps bringing him down the concrete stairs toward me.

"Yes." Forcing a smile, I buttoned my suit coat and closed the distance between us to shake his hand. "Pastor Van Dusen?"

"Pastor Bram. Please." He clasped his other hand atop mine and squeezed, his hazel eyes full of warmth. Unnatural peace and light shone in their depths like I begged God for on a daily basis. "And I am a blessed man, indeed. Welcome to your new home."

My new home.

The words should have replaced the emptiness inside me with the joy I had hoped and prayed for, but nothing had been able to fill me with such feelings after the love I'd lost back in high school.

Swallowing hard, I nodded. "Thank you, sir. It's great to be here."

Pastor Bram released my hand and gripped my shoulder like he might to steer a child even though we stood eye to eye at six feet, give or take a half-inch. "Come on in, and I'll show you around."

The church's entryway smelled like every other one I had entered: lemon furniture polish and the sterility of holiness.

Purity.

Other things I strove for every day in my thoughts and heart and had done a damn good job focusing on since rededicating my life to God a few years earlier.

The soles of my shoes squeaked on the immaculate tiled floor as I followed along behind my new pastor. Double glass doors opened into the sanctuary on our right. A blue carpet aisle pointed the way to the simplistic stage with two stairs leading up to an oak pulpit—

"The offices aren't much." Pastor Bram pulled my focus to where we headed. "But they do afford some privacy." He guided me back through a short hallway into a small reception area, a little gray-haired lady standing from behind a tidy desk as we entered. "Mrs. Howard, this is Malachi Foley, our new youth pastor."

Still having to force my smile in return to hers, I stepped forward and shook her hand. "Ma'am."

"Welcome, Pastor Foley."

The title, although earned and paid for by my parents, hadn't ever sounded right in my ears. Perhaps after a few years in the ministry I would accept having accomplished my parents' dream—God's will—for my life. "Malachi, please."

Mrs. Howard nodded. "I've set up everything I could think of on your desk," she said, motioning toward the door on my right, "but just let me know if you need anything else."

"I will, thank you." I dipped my head and followed Pastor Bram into his office on the left.

It was a larger space than I'd expected, but built-in shelves lined two walls, full of books I had studied in college, making it appear narrow. My own textbooks sat boxed in the apartment I'd rented not far outside the community I'd become a part of overnight.

My office, I found out moments later, was smaller than the pastor's, and it didn't feel like home either. I hoped to change that.

In time.

We made our way back to the auditorium, the carpet hushing our footfalls, the pastor's voice muted by the wood paneling along both walls as he filled me in on the history and daily workings of the church. It appeared almost identical to the one I'd grown up in. Oak pews lay on either side of the main aisle, their backs lined with racks to hold hymnals, hardback copies of the King James Bible, and tiny shelf-like holders for plastic communion cups.

The pulpit stood intimidating at the front, the dais it sat atop making it seem as though it loomed over the congregation from a place of authority. The same as the one I had accepted as a child because my parents said to. One I submitted myself to upon admitting my sins and choosing His path.

Leaving the quiet place of worship behind, we descended the stairs opposite the office wing, and the basement space opened up into a large area with tables and chairs stacked against the far wall beside a small kitchen. A few doors stood along either side —classrooms for the younger children.

I imagined the noise of potluck dinners, the scent of burnt coffee and various pasta dishes bringing back memories from my childhood, and my lips curved upward for real. Mom, as an elder's wife, would have been scurrying around in the kitchen, cheeks pink, her curly blonde hair frizzed around her ears like mine would be if I didn't keep it short.

She and Dad had led me in the path of righteousness, attempting to raise me in the best way they knew how.

I'd been the one to fail.

Thankfully, both had gone to the grave without finding out the depths of my depravity.

My smile faded, and I reminded myself of God's

grace and mercy, His forgiveness of sin in order to silence the demons wanting to drag me back to a place of squalor that would damn my soul to hell.

Putting thoughts of my past behind me, I followed Pastor Bram outside and around back to the second building on the church's five-acre plot.

Elkins Bible School occupied the single-story, more modern building where I would also be teaching the high schoolers their Bible classes for the rest of the spring quarter.

My predecessor had passed suddenly, and Pastor Bram had been filling in as their teacher until our paths crossed by word of mouth.

I had needed a job, an escape from my hometown after caring for my ailing father and finishing my internship the summer before. Although only a year out of Bible college, I landed the job courtesy of my best friend in college, Zeke. Pastor Bram's nephew.

A perfect fit, I told myself. Four hours from a house I'd just sold, from a gravesite at the opposite end of my parents' corner of the cemetery, one that drew me but I refused to visit.

Brian.

My childhood friend, my first secret lover, and the one who had paid the price for our sins.

Jaw clenching in attempts to put my past back beneath the blood of the Lamb, I traversed the small Christian school's halls, wondering how the heck they managed to stay running with only fifteen kids in high school and barely double that in the younger grades.

Kindergarten through grade twelve were all in one building—which sat quiet around us since the students congregated for lunch in a cafeteria Pastor Bram didn't bother showing me.

The job hadn't come with great pay, but when did serving God in an honest and holy way ever line a man's pockets with cash?

With my parents' blessing and financial help, I'd sought a life of fortune in Nashville the day after I graduated high school, hoping my worship leading skills would get recognized and my voice would land me a record deal like Brian and I had planned to do together before God took him from me.

Rebellion, sin, had turned out to be a bigger temptation than wanting to honor God with my vocal gift, and I'd slept with every man I could in attempts to forget my first love.

It had taken the deepest reaches of depression to make me realize I wouldn't ever find contentment and peace outside of God's will for my life. I'd enrolled in Bible college at the encouragement of both my parents, but Mom didn't live to see me graduate like I'd promised her I would.

Dad had stuck around a little longer, but just barely.

They'd had me later in life, and as an only child,

I'd been lavished with unconditional love. Acceptance and grace. Mercy when God hadn't shown it to Brian.

A flicker of gut-wrenching anger lit deep inside my soul, one I fought whenever thoughts of my past rose to the choking point.

I tried to swallow it down with coffee in Pastor Bram's office, courtesy of Mrs. Howard, praying for the Holy Spirit to fill me, to take the hovering despair away.

"We would love to have you join us for dinner this evening, unless you have other plans," Pastor Bram offered.

That was the last thing I felt like doing after a long day of driving and unpacking, but I didn't believe turning my new pastor down would be the right choice. "I appreciate the invitation—thank you."

"I hope you don't mind that my nephew told me about your battle with depression." No pity, no condemnation for my inability to trust God at times, showed on Pastor Bram's face.

"Zeke helped see me through my darkness," I had no issue admitting. My college roommate for all four years knew everything in my past—and he'd never once judged me.

"My son..." Pastor Bram's voice faded off as he peered out his office window to the budding trees beyond. "He's struggling, and I believe God led you here to steer him in the right path."

I met Pastor Bram's gaze as his head swung toward me, my stomach tightening again at the sudden expectation placed on my shoulders. "In the same way I did?"

"No. Rebelliousness." The pastor shifted on his chair and glanced at a five-by-seven photo on his desk facing him. "Isaac is at that age where he doesn't talk much with his mom or me. But he writes a lot of dark poetry, words that don't make sense. It's an outlet." The pastor shrugged, but the frown on his face revealed his true thoughts. He hated that his son would rather take pencil to paper than explain his feelings to his father.

Considering my own emotions had been brushed off when I was younger by my parents and our pastor in order to "trust God," I wasn't surprised the young man didn't share anything of substance with his father.

"He had a strong dislike of our last youth pastor," Pastor Bram continued when I couldn't think of a comment that would sound God-like, "and I'm praying your younger age will help forge a connection between the two of you. I'm hoping you'll take him under your wing. Be a positive influence. Show him what it means to trust God as the Bible commands."

"Of course." I didn't hesitate to agree. Touching

teens' lives had become my mission. I prayed that one day seeking God's will for my life would fill the hollowness in my chest that Brian's death had left behind.

Zeke, my college buddy, had been the only one to know about my past. Oftentimes, Mom had studied the way Brian and I interacted, and I wondered if she knew about the lies I told to cover our sins. She never confronted us, never judged. It was my understanding that my parents had gone to the grave believing I'd gone on to live a holy life while in Nashville, that I'd been saving myself for a godly young woman, a wife to complete me.

But no such woman existed unless she had a dick between her thighs.

Why would God allow such desires—

I cut off the thought as always. Homosexuality was a sin, a result of the fall of mankind. God wasn't to blame for my daily temptation. While I would never consider my sexuality a blessing as a chance to reveal God's strength in me for abstaining, I placed my hope in His ability to guide me toward purity.

Daily prayer and submerging myself in the Word had kept me on His path throughout my college years.

It was time to trust Him for my first ministry too.

———

Pastor Bram's wife Annabelle barely reached my chest in height. I'd learned over our coffee that the tiny Korean woman had been rescued from poverty by the pastor when he'd been on a missions trip overseas twenty-some years earlier.

Dark eyes and dimples. Pretty for a woman and sweet as anything, she welcomed me into their home that night, her demure dress typical of a middle-aged pastor's wife, exactly like I'd expected.

I wore jeans and a light blue hoodie rather than the suit I'd sweated through earlier in the day while settling into my office. Not exactly pastor threads, but outside of the office and church, I didn't feel the need to play the part clothing-wise. A piece of me clung to my college ways, the comfort of jeans, worn sneakers, and T-shirts.

Ties sucked ass—

"Isaac!" Pastor Bram hollered up the stairs, his booming voice bringing my thoughts back from a path leading to darkness.

Footsteps sounded from the second floor, heavier as they approached the landing above us.

"Gird your loins," Pastor Bram quietly stated, his own face frowning with trouble. "I warned him to behave, but he's been his usual moody self since getting home from school. Perhaps it's best if I leave you to it."

I nodded, trusting his judgement.

Pastor Bram clasped my shoulder and moved

toward the kitchen behind me, and I put on a casual, unintimidating smile.

Seventeen-year-old Isaac, the troubled senior in high school.

The pastor's son who wore old black Vans and jeans with enough holes to act as an air conditioner.

He'd inherited his mother's dark hair, I noted as he descended the stairs farther. His smooth jawline and pouty lips in profile made my groin tighten.

Lord, help me...

My lungs stalled out, smile fading as Isaac reached the first floor and turned to greet me.

Our gazes met and held—and I froze, unable to tear my focus off the depths of his hazel eyes similar to his dad's. Except these were pained and filled with wisdom for one so young.

He had the same pale, smooth skin of his Korean mother.

Stunningly beautiful.

A temptation to my baser instincts, the lure of sin I fought on a daily basis.

"So you're my dad's answer to prayer." He stuck out his hand, continuing to hold my stare. The huskiness in his voice, his sarcastic tone attempted to bring life to my neglected dick.

"I'm just a man like any other," I managed to choke out while clasping his hand. Fire raced across my palm and up my arm—ten times more attraction than any I'd felt for anyone in my twenty-six years.

Isaac took a quick glance down over my body before returning my steady gaze. "*Just a man,* my ass." His quiet murmur barely reached my ears, but his eyes stated a hell of a lot more—and heated me clear through to the marrow.

I yanked my hand away from his as though he'd scorched my flesh, bone-deep.

God, what trouble have you brought me into?

His unlit path hadn't guided me to a new beginning, a home of hope like I'd asked Him for.

He had led me straight into temptation.

I prayed He would deliver me from evil.

2

ISAAC

The new youth pastor was hot as fuck. Blond hair and blue eyes, my weakness when it came to men.

Figured.

And for some reason, I couldn't keep my mouth shut at a crucial time in my life. Usually, I clamped my lips tight, only sharing my real thoughts with paper and pen.

But Malachi Foley? Just the sight of his wide shoulders and the peek of a tattoo beneath his long-sleeve T-shirt while gripping my hand lit sinful lust inside me.

He ripped his hand away from mine, finally tearing his stare off my face.

Guess he'd heard my little grumble about him being way more than just a man in my gay opinion.

Elkin's Bible Church's new youth pastor...I

wondered if Dad had any clue he liked guys as much as I did. I held in a snort. Dad would've never let Malachi set foot into our house if he even got a hint of such sin.

"No wife?" I asked, leaning to my left in order to glance around him into the kitchen/dining room where Mom and Dad readied dinner.

Malachi cleared his throat, smoothing down his shirt in my periphery. "No."

His answer would have swelled my dick if I hadn't jerked off while watching some porn on my cell phone a half-hour earlier.

His blue eyes coasted over my face before his lips flatlined.

Mine followed suit in mutual dislike even if the scent of dryer sheets and subtle aftershave coming off him caused the saliva glands in my mouth to erupt.

Why couldn't I be attracted to some kid in the public school, someone as gay as me?

I was stuck inside my closet though, the door locked up tight. Dad and Mom didn't know, and they wouldn't until the minute I turned eighteen and got the hell out of our hick town where rednecks talked about beating faggots to death.

Mother would be devastated when the day of my escape came. She'd prayed for a child for years, same as Sarah in the Bible.

Thus the name attached to me at birth.

But the second I earned my freedom from their legalistic ways, their beliefs in a fairytale book, I would be gone.

Three months to go...

At least I would have some delicious eye candy to fuel my fantasies until I was unleashed to make my own choices in who I wanted to date and finally fuck.

Mom called us to dinner, and I lingered enough for Malachi to turn first, leaving me to trail behind him and check out the new youth pastor's ass.

The man knew how to wear a pair of jeans. Low on his hips but snug enough to tempt a man if he hadn't worn a shirt.

That ass...

So much for not getting a hard-on.

My heels would look good wrapped around his backside. My dick would look even better buried inside it.

Fuck.

I adjusted myself and quickly slid into my chair across the table from Malachi. Head bowed, I waited for Dad to finish praying a blessing over the food, the hands that prepared it, and the typical bullshit that sounded like drivel in my ears and had since I'd learned my ABCs.

He thanked God for the newest addition to his flock, and on that we could agree—even if I disliked the gorgeous man whose blond eyelashes brushed near his cheekbones without twitching while Dad prayed.

Pious young man. Serious and pure, I didn't doubt.

The idea to fuck with him and dirty his soul rose inside me, and I considered it until Dad ended his prayer seconds later. I dug into the chicken Mom had baked, my decision to tarnish Malachi unmade.

"So you're a senior this year." Malachi didn't ask a question so I didn't bother answering. If he wanted information Dad hadn't already given him, he'd have to insert a question mark like a true Pennsylvanian did by raising their voice at the end of a sentence.

But also, I didn't willingly offer shit about myself to anyone.

Another forkful of chicken landed inside my mouth, and I chewed, checking out the blond stubble on Malachi's jawline and his slightly crooked nose. His full lower lip I wouldn't mind tasting.

"What are your plans after graduation?" he asked.

I could lie to please Mom, but I'd had a shit day thanks to a math test I bombed, and I felt like stirring up trouble. "I'm going to head to Nashville and make a name for myself in the music industry."

Malachi's eyes shuttered—blinked—as Dad, God's man, whispered, "Isaac," with his unhappy tone.

My new youth pastor stared at me, and I ignored Dad's quiet reprimand. Malachi could try to read whatever the hell he wanted to on my face, but I knew how to hide my true thoughts and feelings. I'd been doing it for ten years since I realized I wasn't normal, that I liked boys and not girls.

Dad might preach homosexuality being a sin from his pulpit, but it was no choice for me. There was no separating that part of me any more than the hazel-green color from my eyes.

I wondered if Malachi felt the same—or if he simply attempted to squash his sinful nature when it came to masculinity and dicks.

He cleared his throat, but his voice still rasped when he asked, "You sing?"

"He's amazing with a guitar and has a lovely voice," Mom answered the question for me, a smile in her tone that filled me with warmth.

"One he should be using to praise his God," Dad added his usual condemnation when pointing out my wrong choices. Especially ones pertaining to my refusal to stand on stage Sunday mornings with the worship team.

Get up before a group of people and sing praises to a God I didn't believe in? I might hide my true identity, but I was no fake like some of the others caught up in the emotional high of the Holy Spirit.

Malachi glanced between my parents, without a doubt picking up on how one supported me and the other didn't. Supposed unconditional parental love, another thing preached from the pulpit by my dad who ignored it at home.

I expected to see judgement or maybe even pity in Malachi's eyes when his attention returned to me, but understanding resided in their blue depths. The type that made me feel like he empathized with me, that our hearts somehow reached out on their own and tangibly connected.

Fuck—definitely not what I need and sure as hell not with the man across from me.

I looked away first, my knee bouncing beneath the table as I stuffed another bite of chicken into my mouth.

"So, Bram tells me you met while he was in Korea on a missions trip." Another non-question from those lips I'd probably dream about later that night, but thankfully not directed at me.

He must have noticed my discomfort and turned the conversation elsewhere...perhaps Malachi wasn't so bad after all.

While the adults talked about Dad's first trip to Korea, his and Mom's history, and the rest of the school year ahead of our newest Bible teacher and youth pastor, I worked on a new song in my head. Obscure words only I would know the meaning of, an expression of the unnamed emotions I kept bottled up inside.

Depression, most would call it, stemmed from

having to feign my truth. Having to suppress the want and longing for what my body and soul craved, what science had brought to life inside me.

I thought God was real, but I didn't *believe* it. Not like my dogmatic Dad. How could I when He would allow such a cruel thing as men desiring other men? If there was no God like I'd been taught my whole life, then the lusts of my flesh wouldn't be wrong.

But until I gained my freedom to be who I wanted to be—to be who I *was*—I had to continue living a lie.

And the longer I listened to Malachi and Dad discussing God's will and His path of righteousness that would lead to riches in glory, the more I realized I needed to avoid the young man across the table from me. He knew how to talk the talk of the Christian community, even if I was sure his sexual orientation aligned with mine.

Even if the deepest parts of me wanted to wrap around his soul and take solace in someone who understood what I faced on a daily basis, he was off limits to my heart.

3

MALACHI

Troubled, his father had called him.

Trouble for *me*.

Evasive and too intelligent for his own good, Isaac had caught the attention of my sinful nature, and my curiosity craved to be sated. I'd attempted conversation with him a few times while eating dinner, but his misdirection and one-worded answers only left me hungry for more.

Pastor Bram called me His answer to prayer.

God had led me to Elkins Bible Church.

And I wouldn't fail either of them no matter the pastor's son's beauty.

Titled as rebellious, Isaac and his eyes held no glint of mischief whenever our gazes met. No hint of a smirk over our obvious attraction I would deny until I stood before the pearly gates. And no trace of disrespect in his tone, either.

More of a...passive type resistance of authority when I'd expected lashing out from how his father spoke of him.

I had no clue how to handle such an attitude. Unflappable, my mom would have called him. Sensible, my dad would have added. Both would have loved him as they had Brian even though the two seemed polar opposites.

Isaac was smart.

Too smart.

Too...*everything.*

Strong and independent compared to Brian's tender submission. A leader, not a follower, one who would tempt me into sin and end up paying for it himself—

Lord...

I forced my focus on Isaac to keep from reliving my past.

The pastor's son twisted me up inside, and not just because of his striking looks and hazel eyes that appeared greener like the forest color of his long-sleeved T-shirt. How did his brain work? What thoughts prompted his jumping knee beneath the table that mine itched to mimic? Where had he learned the self-control to hold his tongue?

Had his dad beaten him into mock submission?

I listened as the pastor shared about the flock he led, noting the pride lacing his voice. His wife, Annabelle, worshiped him with her steady focus and smile—no evidence of coerced love on her part. She'd fallen hook, line, and sinker for the man God had blessed her life with, but Isaac clearly held no such sentiment.

Their son with his shifty glances longed for freedom, same as I had at his age.

And I expected he would head for even deeper trouble in a matter of months once he graduated and stepped into the world unknown.

My stomach churned over the possibility of him facing what I had—the heartache, the misdirection—and the choices I'd made once ruined.

Sometimes children needed to set their own paths and learn their own lessons the hard way in order to find truth, and while I didn't wish my past on anyone, I knew Isaac leaving town would be the best thing.

For both of us.

All I could do was pray for his soul and trust God to protect the young man from the evil I'd encountered.

Pastor Bram sent Isaac to ready the fire pit after dinner since the spring night was perfect for sitting outdoors, but I stayed put while Annabelle cleared the table rather than trailing after the young man out to their back yard like my flesh longed to do.

"What are your initial thoughts?" Bram asked, leaning forward, arms crossed atop the white table linen.

My eyes followed the path Isaac had taken through the kitchen toward the back door.

He's hurting and lonely.

He's anxious for his freedom.

He'll be my downfall if I don't "gird my loins."

"I think he's a normal teenage boy who's going to have to find the truth of God for himself," I chose to state instead of voicing my true feelings.

With a heavy exhale, Pastor Bram sat back, lips thinning. "You've gotten a taste of his reluctance to communicate. I'm praying that your instruction will inspire him. That he'll be honest with you about what's in his heart."

I could guess at what was in the young man's heart, and it would take a hell of a lot more than being his youth pastor to get him to open up. That would require friendship.

I'd rather avoid him at all costs to save myself from temptation.

Lead me not...

What choice did I have but to trust Him, even if darkness continued to shroud the path He'd planted my feet upon?

"Maybe he'll be willing to talk to me in private," I suggested rather than taking off for my new apartment like self-preservation urged me to do.

Pastor Bram motioned toward the back door. "Feel free, Malachi. I'll be praying God gives you the words to say."

Best if he prays for God to keep my and his son's souls from burning, I thought while standing, my stomach fluttering as I smoothed my shirt down over my abs.

"We don't stay up much past nine," Pastor Bram said, also rising from his chair, "so if Isaac doesn't flee to his room until after then, feel free to linger as long as God leads. We'll remain inside, allowing the two of you some time alone."

Nodding, I left him to help his wife clean up the dinner dishes.

Lead me not into temptation...

Damn prayer was going to be on repeat until Isaac graduated, I didn't doubt.

He sat across the darkening yard, his back to the house. The fire in front of him outlined his hunched form, bulked by a sweatshirt he'd pulled on before heading outside into the cool, spring night. He didn't turn as I approached through the grass, my sneakers announcing an arrival he couldn't pretend to not hear.

"Hey." I settled into the lawn chair beside him, keeping my attention on the ring of stones and entwining yellow and red flames rising into the sky rather than the face I wanted to hold.

Caress.

Kiss.

"Hey," he grunted a reply, poking at the fire with a stick.

I rubbed my hands down my jean-covered

thighs, more ill at ease and nervous than when I'd taken my senior finals at college the year before.

Isaac's manipulating of the kindling sent a burst of sparks upward.

"Think we can start over?"

He grunted but didn't verbalize a reply.

Letting out a heavy exhale, I decided to just dive right in. "So what makes you think I'm your dad's answer to his prayers?"

He leaned back, a stick resting between his spread thighs, peeks of pale skin through ripped jeans drawing my attention.

I tore my gaze off his legs before my imagination wandered.

"Because I'm a depressed, hurting soul who needs God." Isaac's reply sounded like a canned, repeated phrase rather than his own thoughts.

"Why don't you tell me about yourself in your own words?"

He wouldn't look at me but poked at the fire again. "What do you want to know?"

"What you do for fun in this podunk town. Your hobbies. Passions."

"There isn't anything fun about this town. Hobbies are nonexistent. And there's no point in having passions."

I turned toward him fully, needing to read his face since his tone suggested a wall ten feet thick sat like stone between us. "So, what would you recommend a newcomer do on lonely nights?" I hadn't meant the question to be suggestive, but Isaac tilted his head my way, lifting his eyes to meet mine.

Lust lit between us as quickly as a gasoline-soaked newspaper, tightening my groin and snagging the breath from my lungs.

Isaac's focus dropped to my mouth, and he pinched at his lower lip with well-manicured fingernails as though attempting to draw my attention to its natural pout. The brat did it on purpose—and it worked. "You tell me, Pastor Foley."

"Malachi," I rasped what I wanted him to call me —what I wanted to hear him groan while burying my cock deep inside his body, marking him with my scent, my cum—

I cleared my throat and shifted on the rickety chair before tearing my gaze off of sin personified.

"My dad wouldn't allow such blatant disrespect as to call you by your first name," Isaac stated quietly, his tone bland, but I couldn't look at him to read if his face revealed more.

"My dad wouldn't have either." I swallowed hard, expecting I needed to find common ground between us in order to connect outside of my attraction for him. "Like you, I was an only child. Prayed for. A gift."

His soft snort reached my ears—I'd never considered my life a gift either, no matter how many times my parents had assured me of their truth. It seemed another tether sprang to existence between us.

Scuffing the ground beneath my sneaker, I wondered how much would be too much to share. Isaac seemed the sort who would end up learning by living rather than hearing of someone else's mistakes, exactly as I'd told his dad.

But uncovering my sins might invite unwanted advances.

Unwanted.

Don't lie to yourself...

"So you sing?" I went for the next thing I'd learned about him over dinner that had made me want to relate with him.

"Here and there," he said with a shrug.

"The second I was old enough, my father pushed me to join the praise and worship team at our church."

I could feel Isaac's gaze as I stared into the flames.

"It was an outlet for me but not enough. I wanted more. The fame, the money." I bit the words off, clenching my jaw against heading down memory lane. It came anyway, churning my bowels and knifing renewed grief through my chest.

"What happened?" His voice hinted at actual interest, but I'd bonded with him enough for one night.

Still, I couldn't find the strength to leave.

"Long story," I said, thinking on how I'd pushed Brian into sharing my dream and had lost him for eternity. "It's one I'd rather not relive."

Isaac accepted my desire to not share, intensifying the connection I felt simmering between us.

"You remind me of someone I used to know," I admitted before giving it proper thought. Similar through the emotional response they evoked inside me at least, not by personality and definitely not looks. Brian had been a blond with eyes the color of grass in summertime, not dark like Isaac.

"Old boyfriend?"

My head whipped Isaac's way. His hint of a smirk highlighted by firelight was like a kick to my gut.

"Friend," I rasped, hating how easily Isaac got beneath my skin and made me want things I'd left behind.

"If you say so, *Malachi*."

My name on his lips... Disrespectful, according to his father, but ignored. I couldn't begin to imagine what other rules and truths the young man might set aside in order to get what his eyes suggested he wanted.

Isaac Van Dusen would be more trouble than I'd imagined.

I feared for my soul.

4

ISAAC

And Malachi thought he was there to save me from damnation.

I almost snorted again.

The hot piece of ass sitting in Dad's lawn chair had to stop lying to himself. What better way for me to help him see that than fucking with him? Even in the darkening sky, I could tell Malachi's pupils swelled at hearing me call him by name. Add in the emphasis, the hint of a groan I'd inflected in my voice, and the poor man just about came undone.

Breath audibly caught, he stared at my mouth where I'd pinched it to see how he'd react—exactly as I'd wanted. Considering my imagination, I wondered how far his own mind went.

Greedy kisses, grasping hands—his on me, mine on him...

Fuck, how I wanted to experience it rather than just sneaking porn while shut up in my room.

Naked hunger filled his eyes, and I silently thanked all things unholy he hadn't appeared so damn readable inside in front of my parents at the dinner table.

"Tell me more about your friend."

A muscle ticked in Malachi's jaw before he turned to gaze at the fire, the minutes dragging as he seemed to consider opening up to me in the way I knew he—and Dad—hoped I'd do with him.

Something he'd never accomplish in a million years.

"He died when we were seniors in high school," he finally said, and I realized I'd held my breath.

I expected a shit ton more lay behind his single shared line, but I wouldn't push for a story he didn't want uncovered any more than I did my own inner workings. That didn't keep me from staring at him until he shifted on the chair again though.

Maybe if I made him uncomfortable enough, he'd leave me alone so I could go back to living undisturbed in my corner of the world.

But my dick had other ideas.

Malachi leaned down and picked up a small stick off the ground before I could think of other ways to make him squirm, to keep him close so I could continue living in my lust. "Your dad said you write poetry."

I narrowed my gaze, studying how the fire's light glinted off the gold highlights of his short hair as he snapped the twig in two. "What of it?" I asked, my fingers itching to run over the wavy strands.

Mine weren't ramblings like Dad always called them, but I wasn't about to admit the truth of what my journals held.

"Is that how you express your feelings?" Malachi glanced at me, keeping his focus on my eyes rather than my lips. His quick study of my face and the obvious want in his blues tightened my groin.

"With words?" Not that I needed clarity, but my notebooks, my songs, weren't something I shared with anyone, even if Malachi had attempted to do what I dreamed about with my life.

He paused before answering, seemingly lost in his past, with his focus on the firepit. "I knew a song-writer once."

"That friend of yours?"

Malachi tossed one of the sticks into the flames. "He struggled to express what was in his head, so he took pen to paper. Created magic with those words."

Again, I expected more lay behind his story, but my new youth pastor was about as open as I was.

"He planned to go to Nashville, same as me." Malachi's voice broke off abruptly, and I focused on the ground between my old Vans, allowing him the moment he obviously needed. The other stick he'd held arced through the air in my periphery to land with a burst of sparks in the fire.

An ex-boyfriend, if I had to guess from his obvious torment...maybe losing him was what had turned him toward God.

I wondered if that was why he'd taken interest in me and followed me outside.

Frowning, I poked at the fire again. Chances were, even if he did admit to wanting me, I wouldn't ever compare to the ghost that owned Malachi Foley. Same as I wouldn't ever be good enough in Dad's eyes.

What was the point of trying?

My semi I'd been dealing with all night wilted, and my scowl deepened.

"It's not a sin to have ambitions, Isaac." He finally broke the silence between us, his voice resigned as fuck. "But it's the choices you make in pursing what you want that will mold your future."

"That friend of yours never got a chance to pursue his, did he?"

A muscle ticked in his jaw as he stared unblinking at the dying flames. "No."

"Nothing's going to stop me," I stated with the same conviction Dad did while spewing his thoughts on homosexuality and sin from the pulpit.

"I hope it doesn't." He let out a heavy sigh that physically caused his body to shudder. "Every person should have a chance to fulfill their dreams

—even if it's not exactly what God would have for their life."

He was hurting, no doubt about it. I wanted to reach over and wrap my arms around him, to take his bad memories away. I sat stunned at the weird desire to give him comfort.

"Do you have a cell?" His question seemed out of left field.

"Yeah." I pulled my phone from my back pocket.

"Add me as a contact," he said, and I did as he gave me his number. "Call me—anytime, Isaac. If you need an ear, need to unload...whatever and whenever, I'm available."

An offer of friendship, but the word *unload* had my mind going straight to the gutter and bringing blood and a whole lot of want back to my dick.

A smirk started as I tucked my cell away, but Malachi stood and walked off before I thought up something sarcastic to say to get under his skin.

He bypassed the back porch for the path leading around to the front of the house.

A sense of loneliness swept over me, worse than the usual kind that brought on my depression. Scowling again from the sense I'd lost something, I poked at the fire, stirring the embers to cause flying sparks.

An engine came to life out front and faded into the night, leaving me more alone than I'd ever felt.

For the next two nights in a row, I dreamed of golden hair beneath my fingertips. Biting the full bottom lip of a forbidden man I shouldn't even consider thinking about. Looking into his eyes while he buried himself so damn deep inside my body I couldn't breathe.

Waking with my dick in my hand Sunday morning, I finished myself off the same as the day before, groaning, my hips jerking with every spurt of cum splattering up over my abs.

Shit.

I heaved for breath, holding my length until it softened fully, the memory of Malachi and his scruffed jawline so deeply embedded in my memory I could see him in vivid detail every time I closed my eyes.

Dad had asked me what I'd done to send his youth pastor home Friday night without saying goodbye to them. He didn't believe my lie that we thought they'd gone to bed.

The stern look he gave me when I sat down for breakfast Sunday morning let me know he still didn't.

But when had he ever believed a word I said?

I'd been full of shit as a younger kid, always telling tales to save myself from getting Dad's belt or Mom's wooden spoon.

Stole a piece of a candy? No rod spared.

Didn't do my Bible studies for Sunday school? Belt.

Forgot to place my shoes in the mud room's bin where they belonged? Wooden spoon—and Dad's belt as a second discipline when he got home from his office.

Failure after failure, no matter how hard I tried to do right.

But they wouldn't have to put up with my bullshit for much longer.

Dad took his car to the church early like he did every Sunday while Mom and I ate bagels and cream cheese together in peaceful quietness, both of us showered and ready for a day of listening to the Word and reflection.

Apart from breakfast with Mom, Sundays sucked, and not in the way I wanted to experience for myself—giving and receiving. I wondered while staring out the passenger window as Mom drove us to church if Malachi had any actual experience with swallowing a guy's dick, or if like me, he'd only wished and wondered. If he dreamed and came over thoughts that in Dad's world would condemn us to eternal damnation.

I wanted God to be a farce, a crutch for those too weak to face the reality of death being just that—nothing. A void of darkness, same as before a person's first cognitive thought.

Then I could live my life without question, standing or falling before my own sense of morality rather than a supposed all-knowing being beyond the pearly gates of heaven where a mansion of gold awaited those faithful to His commands.

No such house awaited me and never would.

5

MALACHI

Pastor Bram's flock jammed into the small place of worship, close to two hundred members. Hardly a mega church like I'd been raised in, but the spirit of God seemed to fill the room before service started. Kindness greeted me with every introduction, and even though I felt the stares of the congregation while I sat on stage with our pastor, I didn't get a sense of judgement over the new, *young* youth pastor.

If they'd known my past, things would have been different.

Of a young enough age to catch the interest of the tittering high school girls, I should have preened at their obvious attention, but it was the blatant stare of darkly-lashed hazel eyes that had me shifting on my seat.

How a boy of seventeen managed to unhinge my

mind so easily baffled me. No one had made me question my upbringing and my sense of right and wrong since Brian.

Isaac Van Dusen.

Thoughts and dreams of him over the weekend had filled me with an unholy craving I wished I could loathe.

I wanted inside his head. I wanted to know his thoughts, the dark words he wrote in his journal. I wanted his body beneath me, his moans and whimpers in my ears.

Damnit.

Jaw clenched, I forced my focus to remain on the pastor God had led me to labor beside, to submit to.

Just a few months...I could handle this temptation with constant prayer.

If only I felt like praying with the same urgency I felt for jerking off to fantasies about the pastor's son.

After the service, I stood at the back of the church by the doors leading out into the warm morning, shaking hands with everyone who passed by.

The hairs on my arms rose beneath my suit coat, but I didn't glance toward the group of young men hanging by the auditorium's entrance. Annabelle came through the receiving line, inviting me to have lunch with them, but I declined with a smile, thanking her all the same.

I had shit to do—not that I used those exact words.

In my periphery, I kept track of her son moving off toward a side exit. My breath eased as he disappeared outside, but my chest stung. For all the attention he'd given me during the service, I'd expected a clashing of gazes or a handshake held a few seconds too long.

I'd looked forward to it, I realized as the metal door slammed behind him and his friends, taking his energy from the building and leaving me behind.

Keeping my smile fixed in place and ignoring the drop of my stomach, I greeted those behind Annabelle, including the young woman who helped with the youth group.

She was single.

A cute brunette with big doe-like eyes.

But nothing about her tempted me like Isaac did.

"It's nice to finally meet you!" She smiled, joy lighting her face and causing her eyes to twinkle. Attraction for me or an outward manifestation of God's love, I couldn't decide. Either way, I wasn't interested. "I'm Jennifer, your partner in crime with the teens. I also teach music at the school."

"Malachi," I replied, shaking her hand.

"I'm sorry I haven't been around since you arrived," she said, glancing at the people still waiting to greet the newcomer. "I was out of town. But." She let go of my hand and grasped her purse in front of her. "I'll stop by your office tomorrow to fill you in on the upcoming retreat."

"Sounds good," I murmured with a nod, not unkindly, but zero trace of interest inflected my eyes and voice.

"Is ten okay? Neither of us have class at that time."

"I'll be in my office."

She smiled again and moved onto Pastor Bram as the next in line greeted me.

Why couldn't I be attracted to someone like her? Why couldn't the bubbly young woman hugging Annabelle after Pastor Bram with a sparkle in her dark eyes draw me in like Isaac did?

Why, God? Why allow such feelings, such want in a man's soul if it's a sin?

My throat tightened, and my feet grew restless, my legs needing to flee. I longed to hop in Dad's truck and escape to my small apartment, to soak in the quietness while praying for God to fill the emptiness in my chest.

Fifteen long as hell minutes later, I managed to do just that, sweats and a T-shirt replacing the restrictive suit I'd worn to church. A frozen tray of my favorite lasagna cooked in the microwave, and I leaned against the counter with both hands, watching the turntable slowly spin, the whine of the machine static in my ears.

All my lunch had to do was sit there and let fate

have her way. Manipulating its movement, the microwave changed the cells inside to heat it through so the food could be consumed without causing illness.

I wished God would take over in such a way, to finish the work he'd started in me, but prayer wouldn't come to ask Him to remove my burden and guide me through life.

As God's children, we were called to hate the sin and love the sinner—but I couldn't find hatred for the part of me that defined who I'd been since high school.

I was as gay as the winter nights were dark. There was no denying that truth.

Anger stirred inside me whenever I thought too long on where God's mercy had been when allowing such sins to come about, but the microwave dinged, keeping me in the present.

Famished, I sat at the small table and stared at my lunch, wondering what Annabelle had served her family and what I'd missed out on by declining her invitation.

"Probably fifty times more appetizing than this shit," I muttered and immediately asked forgiveness in my head for swearing even though I loved frozen lasagna and didn't feel the curse word shit deemed the need for repentance.

My cell rang, and I left my untouched lunch

behind to retrieve the phone from where I'd placed it on my dresser.

Zeke.

Grinning, I swiped to answer, true happiness coming over me for the first time in weeks. "What's up, Ezekiel?"

"Asshole." My best friend from college and newly certified Christian counselor hated his full name.

I chuckled. "What's going on?"

"How was your first day with the new flock?" he asked rather than answering.

"Good," I replied on auto pilot, settling back at the table where my steaming lunch waited. "Your uncle Bram seems pretty cool. The congregation was very welcoming."

"Any hot women?"

Of course his mind went straight to what we'd both hoped for—for my sake.

"Not a one," I answered truthfully, my smile flatlining.

"Men?"

Zeke was the only one on the face of the earth other than those I'd fucked during my wild days in Tennessee who knew what drew my attention. He'd also heard all about my daily struggles with the sin rooted deep inside me and my inability to find the female form attractive.

The hollowness inside my chest expanded over

my failures, and I let out a heavy exhale, my eyes falling closed. "Isaac."

"Oh fuck."

I pinched the bridge of my nose, knowing Zeke probably did the same. "Why would He lead me to a place of temptation like this, Zeke?" My voice wavered on the edge of cracking.

"To give Him glory."

A canned response, one I'd expected from a man trained to walk the walk and talk the talk. He'd been raised in a mega church himself up near Boston.

"I'm on a path with no light," I muttered. "An unseen track I'm aimlessly stumbling down." I sat back and slouched in my chair.

"You need to give your weakness to God."

"I've offered it up hundreds of time," I snipped out, my hand fisting on the table beside my cooling food.

"Faith is the evidence of things unseen," Zeke said quietly, and I wished I could hate how easily he stated truth when I fought to even convince myself of it.

"Blindly trusting I'm doing the right thing isn't a pleasant experience," I grumbled.

"God will reveal his will for you in time—you know that."

Did I?

I longed to agree, to understand, and experience the same emotional sense those in worship had earlier that morning at church. They'd raised hands while singing praises, their inner peace and joyful countenances covet-worthy.

Except for the handful of teens who appeared bored out of their skulls, one especially I'd refused to look full in the face.

Isaac struggled like I did, but not being in a position of authority left him free to say and do what he wanted.

I swallowed hard over the confession about to pour from my lips. "He makes me feel things I haven't since Brian."

"Shit."

Zeke might be a spiritual guy who loved helping hurting souls, but swearing proved his daily struggle. Raised by reformed heathens with sailor-like mouths, my best friend often dealt with issues from his early years before finding God.

If only mine were a lot less depraved like his.

"I'm not sure how well you know him?" I asked.

"I haven't seen Isaac since he was around ten."

"He's rebellious and quietly owns his sexuality." I filled Zeke in. "Has beautiful expressive hazel eyes he doesn't bother shielding."

"Is my uncle aware?"

"If I had to guess, I'd say no." I let out another audible exhale. "Pastor Bram just said he's shut off. Quiet. Won't share anything with either of them."

"Sounds like someone I know."

"Yeah." I pushed aside my lunch, kicked my legs out straight, and thoroughly sank back in my chair, eyes closing again. "Reminds me of me." Straight down to the independent, driven spirit.

"What helped put you on the right path?" Zeke asked, even though he was well aware of every detail from that time.

"Hitting rock bottom."

"Sounds like my little cousin needs to get out on his own and live his life. Make mistakes and find God."

"He's graduating in May and turns eighteen in July." I might have looked at his school records so I could count down the days until he took off to chase his dreams like he said he planned on doing.

"So three months."

"Give or take a couple weeks, yeah."

"God placed you in Elkins for a reason, Malachi. The doors opened up for you to step into that role there—those kids need you, the school needs you. Whatever the reasons, He'll see you through. You have to trust Him in that."

I wanted to—hell, how I wanted to live the truth my parents had held close in their hearts.

"Do your thoughts ever stray?" I opened my eyes as Zeke hesitated in answering.

Zeke found women attractive—but sometimes men caught his eye too. But unlike me, he'd never gone down that road. His secret sin had only been in his mind—he'd never felt the clench of a forbidden hole grasping at his dick, sucking his length into tight heat. He'd never shot his spunk over a man's tongue, holding a masculine jaw while unloading.

My dick swelled, and grimacing, I squeezed the base in an attempt to keep from thickening fully.

"They do," Zeke finally spoke. "But when temptation to taste that sin enter my head, I get on my knees and lay them before the throne of God."

Those straying ideas used to send me to my knees for a completely different reason. One I enjoyed, that used to make me feel powerful. Sexy.

"I gotta go," I rasped, memories and new fantasies taking me past the point of no return. It'd been too long, and my balls filled with an ache I knew from experience I wouldn't be able to pray away.

"I'll lift you up in prayer," Zeke promised quietly. "Call me if you need me."

"Yeah." I hung up, needing a hell of a lot more than a friend's ear.

I tossed aside my cell and slid my sweats down to let my aching dick have some freedom. It was fully swollen, and a bead of precum welled at the slit. Thoughts of Isaac on his knees for me, lips parted and waiting to taste me pulled my balls up tight against my groin.

Groaning, powerless over my sin, I smeared the

droplet around my palm and fucked up into my hand.

"Fuck," I cursed between clenched teeth, slowly jacking myself, all thoughts of God demolished from my head.

I imagined glinting hazel eyes. Nostrils widening as I pressed deep into Isaac's throat, cutting off his oxygen. Tears welling, drool smearing.

I wanted to grasp his hair, fuck into his throat, and soak in his whimpers while he jerked himself—got off over pushing me past the point of sanity.

Cum erupted up through my length, splattering my T-shirt, my wrist...a full week's worth I'd been holding back, refusing myself.

In my opinion, masturbation as a form of release to a virile man celibate for almost five years couldn't be wrong. But to thoughts of a beautiful young man who hadn't yet reached adulthood? Legal in the state of Pennsylvania, but still off limits. Never mind the fact he had a dick of his own between his thighs rather than a vagina I couldn't even think about without grimacing.

Gay.

Thoroughly.

A sinner.

Sucking oxygen, I eyed the globs of white coating my hand and soaking my shirt rather than dripping from a gaping hole I wanted to taste.

"Dammit." Ripping my shirt off overhead, I stood, my gut hard and my throat tight.

Lunch remained where I'd pushed it, untouched, and I hopped in the shower to wash myself.

My cum disappeared down the drain—if only I could cleanse my soul of sin so easily.

6

ISAAC

I sported a hard-on all through church and made sure to avoid Malachi after the service ended. Me and two kids from the youth group I hung out with on occasion, Chris and Tyler, snuck out the side door and lingered at the back of the parking lot until my mom made her way to our car.

Dad would be home after locking up which left me with a good half-hour to milk my balls dry while Mom finished preparing lunch.

It took all of ten seconds from the time I locked myself in the bathroom to come, my fist around my dick as I imagined Malachi fondling me.

"Shit," I gasped out, the second shot more a dribble into the toilet I stood in front of. Zero evidence that way, unlike a ball of tissues—couldn't have Mom finding out I enjoyed jerking off as much as I did. She'd tell Dad, then I'd get the lecture about masturbation being a sin and that I shouldn't be touching myself while having lustful thoughts about women.

If they only knew the truth.

Huffing a snort of laughter, I tucked myself away, washed up, and went out to help Mom, feeling relieved but far from relaxed.

"So, what do you think of the new youth pastor?" she asked while setting the plates on the table. I followed along behind with the flatware, my body still tingling from the aftereffects of busting a nut.

"He's cool, I guess."

Hot as fuck. Fantasy fodder.

"Your father really likes that he's younger. I'm sure he'll connect better with the youth group."

I grunted a non-committal noise she could take however she wanted. While Mom was easier to talk to than Dad, the less I said, the better off I'd be. If Mom caught on to the truth about me, she would tell Dad.

Couldn't have that shit.

"I know you don't like to share your inner workings, Isaac," she said, softly touching my shoulder.

I placed Dad's fork and knife down without looking at her even though her affection warmed my insides.

"But I can see you're struggling. Maybe Malachi could help."

"You want me to go to him for counseling?" I

didn't need to ask—I'd overheard my parents speaking about that very thing the night before.

"I'm just suggesting that you could use a friend, one who has your best interest and God's will in mind."

If Malachi's eyes indicated anything, he didn't have either of those interests in his mind. He might believe God's will was what he ought to think about, but the strong vibes between us couldn't be denied.

He wanted me under his hands.

I wanted his hands *on* me.

But he was also a godly man determined to do right. The clenched jaw and the blatant way he'd ignored me all morning during church solidified that truth in my head.

"I'll try," I lied to Mom, knowing I could never do such a thing. Malachi might want to fuck me, but his God would always come first. I didn't need to make myself vulnerable only to end up disappointed.

Best to wait to experience all my firsts once I escaped my prison bars and could stretch my wings and fly.

I had Bible class first period, and what a way to start off the day. Malachi sat at the teacher's desk when I walked in. His button-down blue dress shirt matched the color of his eyes with the sleeves rolled up to expose vein-lined forearms with a tree tattoo I'd only caught a hint of prior.

I wondered if Dad knew he'd gotten inked—but Malachi's gaze pinned me in place, stealing my breath and causing me to stumble to a stop in the open classroom door.

Someone bumped into me, pushing me forward.

"Morning," he said, turning his focus on the person behind me—but his rasped tone and the want in his short-lived gaze caused energy to buzz like a zap of lightning through my blood.

I slid into my seat to calm my racing heart and hide the instant chub I sported.

And I'd emptied my balls an hour earlier while in the shower since I would be seeing him for first period.

Rather than listen to his lecture on Paul's letter to the Corinthians, I focused on how Malachi's mouth moved. Lips shaping words, the flash of white teeth, a peek of the tip of his tongue.

Sexy...so damn hot I couldn't even begin to imagine how both would feel on me.

My mind went down the rabbit hole of so-called immorality, and I got so caught up in fantasizing about him getting on his knees for me that I didn't give two shits if someone noticed my lust for our new youth pastor.

I'd hidden my desire for the same sex for years and feared the truth coming to light...but for

Malachi, for a taste of him, the chance to touch...
hell, I'd do whatever it took.

No.

Ripping my focus off his mouth, I frowned at the
Bible in front of me. He would never accept me or
what I wanted. Malachi was a man of God by intent,
and falling for him would only end in my heart
getting crushed beneath his heel. The thought of
making myself vulnerable to that kind of hurt
churned my stomach.

I wouldn't ever give a man power over me like
that. Ever. Dad had dictated my entire childhood—I
wouldn't allow another man to keep me beneath his
thumb.

Best to continue telling myself I didn't like
Malachi. That ignoring his gorgeous blue eyes, the
broad shoulders, and the tattoos on the lower half of
his right arm, no matter how fucking sexy they were
and no matter how hard he made me, would be for
the best.

The second the bell rang, I shot out of my desk
and booked it for the door, sucking in oxygen the
second I escaped the feel of his gaze on my backside.

Did he want to fuck me? Did he imagine holding
me down while claiming what no man had ever
touched?

Fucking hell.

Frowning, I stomped into music class, nodding at
Miss Jennifer when she greeted me with a cheery

smile. While the rest of the students filtered in, I sat in the corner, my mind needing to vomit words, to create something to express the feelings inside me.

I pulled out my latest journal, its pages almost filled with ramblings others wouldn't be able to read or understand. Sometimes dark, sometimes more on the gray side, but all my inner emotions in random phrases.

My writings were the source of Dad and Mom's concern, the reason they wanted me to get counseling.

But I couldn't share what went through my mind. Doing so would bring me out of the closet I had padlocked ten times over.

Three months to go.

My throat tightened while I wrote down sporadic words, ones plucked from the full thoughts in my head. Evidence of my truth but not revelation.

Good thing for me Miss Jennifer's class focused on the outward expression of the Spirit of God working in our lives. Creative writing through music. Definitely a different take on chorus or band like Chris and Tyler over at the public school endured as an elective, but I enjoyed Miss Jennifer's class. It fit with my dreams.

I imagined my guitar in my hands, plucking out chords...the words in front of me stringing along as nonsensical to anyone but me.

Broken.

Wanting.

Filled up...not alone.

Worship—but not in the way Dad preached.

Communion, and not the cracker and grape juice we partook of once a month.

Underneath, all around.

Consumed by raging fire.

I hummed beneath my breath, my fingers moving on my lap as though playing my guitar.

"What are you working on?" Miss Jennifer asked from beside me, jerking me from my dream-like trance.

I cleared my throat and shut my journal. "Just jotting ideas down like you told us to."

She sat in the empty chair beside me. "Have you given any more thought to joining the praise and worship team?"

The idea tempted bile to rise up the back of my throat. I could lie to anyone's face about who I was. But to stand on stage and sing praises to a God who didn't love mankind created in his image enough to keep lusts of the flesh from entering the world?

No fucking way.

"Nah." I shrugged and glanced around the room at the other kids bowed over their own papers, attempting to create music from the words in their minds.

"You're incredibly talented."

I picked at a hangnail.

"You should be using those gifts for God."

"Maybe someday," I offered even though I would do no such thing. My music teacher was the piano player in our church's praise team, and she'd been on me to join them ever since she'd caught me singing almost ten months earlier.

Had I'd been aware anyone stood within earshot at the youth retreat the summer before, I never would have sung the tune I'd been playing in my head and practicing on my guitar for weeks on end.

She'd told me later she heard the entire song, and while she hadn't understood the lyrics, she recognized my ability to weave music outside the usual three chords of pop music. Intuitive, she'd called me. Artistic and different, both of which I already knew and hinged my dreams on.

"Are you going on the retreat this year?"

I nodded. Dad wouldn't allow me a choice even though I would be a high school graduate when the youth group drove up to Maine in a couple months like it did every summer.

But Malachi would be behind the wheel of the van, and a week-long stint in the deep woods where I wouldn't be able to escape him...

Maybe I would pretend to be sick. No fucking way could I be in a bunk room with him lying mere feet away.

No. Fucking. Way.

"I know you aren't comfortable with performing in front of people—"

She had that part wrong—I lusted for it almost as much as I did Malachi.

"—but starting out in a small group like the one heading to Maine would be a good beginning. Will you at least bring your guitar along again this year?"

I shrugged, figuring I could find some time alone to work on my songs. "I guess so."

At least at camp I could sing whatever the hell I wanted and not get chastised for them being non-Jesus songs. Anything Dad didn't recognize as praising God wasn't allowed in his house.

"I would love to send a demo of yours to my cousin."

My focus jerked toward her face. "The one in Nashville?"

"Yes." Miss Jennifer smiled, excitement in her eyes. "He's been searching for up-and-coming talent. I think he'd really like your music. It's unique, something I haven't heard on Christian radio before."

Probably because nothing about my lyrics suggested a Christian wrote it. Guess my song from last summer had been cryptic enough that she didn't have a clue.

Boy, would her cousin be disappointed in learning the truth about my ramblings.

"I'm not really ready for something like that," I finally answered, at a loss for what else to say. What aspiring musician turned down that kind of offer? But I couldn't fake who I was.

Miss Jennifer patted my shoulder. "When you are, Isaac, I'd love to sit and hear more of your work. It's groundbreaking."

She left me, and my gaze trailed after her as she went to the next kid to see what they wrote about. A great girl. If only I was a dick enough to take advantage of what she offered.

A foot in the door. Maybe make some connections...but I couldn't use my music teacher like that. She was too sweet, and I didn't expect her cousin would want an openly gay musician signing with the Christian label he worked for.

Well, openly gay once I struck out on my own.

July and my birthday couldn't come soon enough.

7

————

MALACHI

Ten o'clock on the nose and a knock sounded on my office door.

"Come in!"

Jennifer did as bid, smiling like always with the joy of Jesus on her face.

Guilt weighed my body heavier into my seat. Catching Isaac's gaze when he'd walked into class had thrown me for a damn loop. Took my brain off the lecture I'd planned for my first day of class with the high schoolers. I'd struggled through my first two classes before break.

And I couldn't find the ability to make myself pray and ask for help.

"How were the kids this morning?" Jennifer sat primly on the chair across from me, hands clasped lightly on her lap. A fifties-like dress covered her from neck to below her knee, but even if she'd been in a tight, low-cut blouse and short pencil skirt, she wouldn't have gotten a rise out of me.

Such a shame.

"Good," I stated and cleared my throat, straightening some papers on my desk. "They were all well behaved and listened better than I'd expected." Except for Isaac. He had stared at me, making me uncomfortable in my own damn skin. I doubted he'd heard a word I said if his eyes portrayed what went through his head.

The same thing I'd fantasized about, the craving that grew with every inhale in his skin-tingling presence.

"We've really been blessed with an awesome group of kids the past couple of years." Jennifer's voice was too damn bubbly.

I need more coffee, I told myself, *not the pastor's son.*

"Hardly any drama with the girls and no fights between the boys," Jennifer continued. "But with the Maine trip, being in close proximity for a few days without a break will bring in a bit of both. It always does."

The Maine trip to a youth hostel in the woods near Moose Head Lake would be a place to labor for the Lord with our acts of servitude. Painting. Landscaping. A chance for the kids to semi-vacation without watchful parents. An opportunity to explore in dark corners or behind trees the things they wouldn't attempt at home.

I'd been such a kid once. Me leading Brian into the darkness...

"Are you alright?"

"Hmm?" I lifted my focus to Jennifer, whose brow had furrowed. Guess I'd sat frowning at my desk too long. "Yeah." I forced a smile. "Just remembering my own youth group trips."

Her smile returned. "The singing around the campfire is always the best. S'mores. Silly ghost stories and laughter."

"Sounds like a good time."

"It is." Her smile remained as she studied me until I shifted in my seat.

"So it looks like everything is all set for June," I said, picking back up the file for the upcoming trip that my predecessor had already pretty much handled.

"I'm sending out consent forms and waivers next week," Jennifer said. "We require the parents for those kids attending to sign them."

I nodded, knowing how things had changed since I'd been in the youths' shoes. "So there are two large rooms, one for the girls and one for the guys," I repeated what I'd read in the file.

"Yes."

"Have there been any issues with kids sneaking out in the past?"

"Once," Jennifer said, her cheeks turning pink.

I raised an eyebrow, waiting for her to expand.

"Um...I was the guilty party."

My other eyebrow lifted. "You?" I couldn't believe it.

"Yes." She glanced away, her guilt obvious even though a good ten years must've passed since her graduation. "Me and my boyfriend at the time decided we didn't want to wait for marriage, and we snuck out of the rooms once everyone slept."

I stared, struck dumb. Sweet, bubbly Jennifer Sutton, godly woman who served the Lord... "You had sex," I sputtered. "Outdoors. While on a youth trip?"

She gasped, her eyes widening. "Oh my goodness, no! Just kissed. I would never!"

Kissed... *Holy hell.* I barely held in my burst of laughter. "You mean to tell me you weren't going to kiss a guy until marriage?"

"No-touch love is the best way to keep your purity until marriage."

I stared, my smile fading. What the hell did they preach at Elkin's Bible Church? No-touch love. Abstinence from...everything? Shit, I couldn't imagine being a horny teenager and not even feeling you had the right to kiss the person you crushed on.

"Does the no-touch love teachings include holding hands?" I had to ask.

"Once you're engaged, it's allowed."

What kind of church had I submitted myself to? Not that I wanted to hold a woman's hand or kiss her lips, but still. Talk about restrictive as fuck—even more so than the Bible church I'd grown up in.

"Have you heard the pastor's son sing?"

Her one-eighty question caught me off guard. "Huh?"

"Isaac. He's got an incredible voice. I'm hoping I can get him to share his gift while we're in Maine. I caught him singing while hiding away last year, and let me tell you, that boy is talented beyond words."

"His mom mentioned it, yes," I replied, remembering all too well how she'd supported his dreams while his dad didn't. A situation I'd seen before with Brian, the heartbreak of which I'd attempted to soothe.

Memories flashed in my head of me and Brian cuddled together, our voices in perfect harmony, and my promises afterward to stand by his side when the time came for us to leave for Nashville.

I cleared my throat, pushing against the past, against the similar connection I felt with Isaac.

"He's *so* good," Jennifer gushed. "I'm dying to send a demo to my cousin down in Nashville."

Pausing in shuffling papers on my deck, I glanced up at her. "Your cousin is in the music industry?"

"Elliot James."

Oh, holy hell. The blood drained from my face, leaving me feeling light-headed as fuck. "*The* Elliot James?" I managed to ask.

"One and the same." Jennifer beamed, and I wondered if she considered pride as much of a sin as breaking the no-touch love teachings.

But Elliot...

A bi-man who hid his truth. A guy who'd been interested in me as a gay virgin and not because of my talents. All it had taken was hints of his interest in signing me on with his label, and I'd gotten on my knees for him. Twice. Once to give him my mouth, and the second time to give him my ass. The second had been a first for me since Brian and I hadn't gone beyond mutual hand and blow jobs. Painful yet hot, Elliot's and my passion had burned as bright as the stars.

Naive and innocent, I'd thought it had been love, the man who would heal me from my loss of Brian.

However, Elliot had kicked me out of his fancy apartment in downtown Nashville immediately after taking my virginity like I'd done something wrong.

Talk about a damn insecurity feeder—and the beginning to my complete downfall.

"Do you know him?" Jennifer asked.

Intimately.

"No," I forced out the lie and cleared my throat again, pushing aside thoughts of my further failure, how I'd gone on to other beds and dark hallways in my rebelliousness. I'd given it up once, so why hold back? Luckily, God had protected me during those years, and physically, I'd escaped unscathed. "I know *of* him, but not him personally."

Oh, the deception...if Jennifer asked her cousin about me, would he uncover our sins? Blab the truth of my past and ruin the path I'd chosen because of my promise to Mom on her deathbed? Doing so, though, would reveal his sexual preferences too, and as a big exec in the Christian music industry, I expected he'd want to keep that shit under wraps.

"He would sign Isaac in a heartbeat," Jennifer mused.

My blood pressure rose, probably bringing color back to my face. He'd try to fuck the boy too, I didn't doubt. I'd heard through the grapevine he took advantage of other dreamers like I'd been once upon a time.

"Pastor Bram wouldn't approve of a demo," I stated with a stern voice even as my hands fisted atop my desk. The last thing I could imagine was Isaac giving up his firsts—if he hadn't already—to a man bent on stealing them with alluring, false claims.

"You don't think?"

"No."

Jennifer let out a sigh at my hard tone, even though I didn't know if I spoke the truth or not. "He's just so, so talented—gifted, I mean," she hastened to correct herself that God was the giver of Isaac's voice.

Her words made my mind whirl. Yet another

thing Isaac and Brian—and *I*—had in common. Another connection that could easily sway me toward the young man when I needed to keep my distance.

"He just needs to overcome his insecurity so I can get him to help with the praise and worship team," Jennifer said with a sigh as though her thoughts on Isaac's situation, her *truth*, was the absolute answer. "He needs to let go, and let God."

My stomach twisted at Jennifer's canned words, a cliché phrase I'd heard hundreds of times in various churches. Let go of the old man, the inherent sinful nature, and let God have his way.

She obviously didn't struggle like I did to accept what had been spoon-fed to me since childhood.

I walked her out of my office a few minutes later after going over last-minute retreat plans, grabbed that coffee I needed, and headed back to the school building behind the church.

At least I wouldn't have to see Isaac in class for the rest of the day.

8

ISAAC

Miss Jennifer followed Malachi around like a lost puppy, but what single woman in her twenties wouldn't? His presence couldn't be ignored, and his vivid light eyes drew a damn soul in with an intensity that hitched breaths and pinkened countless cheeks.

But not a single female got under his skin like I could.

One suggestive glance was all it took to fluster my Bible teacher. And at Wednesday night youth group? He couldn't even look at me, no matter how silently I begged him with my sharp gaze to give me the time of day.

But I didn't want his attention.

Not really.

At least, I told myself that, considering he was too religious like my dad.

The evil part of me, hidden in the deepest reaches, wanted to soil his purity. Break down the fake-ass walls he'd put up as a front. I lusted to see him dirtied in the eyes of my dad who couldn't keep from singing his praises as if telling me how awesome Malachi was would make us friends.

And seeing Malachi smile, relaxed and at ease with Miss Jennifer, pissed me off. Unguarded, he seemed open with her when he didn't realize I was around, watching him like a fucking creepy stalker.

Perhaps the reason he'd made it a point to ignore me was because he hated me. Or maybe the attraction between us sickened him.

He wanted a godly woman, not the too-young pastor's son who dreamed of dick.

Malachi preached acceptance in Bible class on Tuesday and Wednesday. He showed mercy to one of the ninth graders who hadn't gotten their homework turned in on time. But me?

He treated me as though I didn't exist, and I hated it like the little brat I couldn't help but be.

On our second Wednesday night with the new youth pastor, I sat in our school's gymnasium with my friends Chris and Tyler. I knew I could rile the two guys up since they usually stirred trouble when pushed. While waiting for Malachi to get started with the night's lesson, I shot the shit with them and got them talking about girls.

Whispers and snickers of which ass they'd

tapped, the latest party they'd been to. How much they drank, who I needed to hook up with if I wanted to get high—them. While I could care less about pussy, for the sake of making waves, I could definitely pretend I did.

"What about the Burns girl?" I asked, leaning in, my voice lowered so no one would hear with the other clamor going on around us from the metal folding chairs.

"Lindy?"

"Yeah. The blonde with the huge tits," I whispered what I'd heard them talk about the week before. "Either of you had a taste of her?"

Chris snorted, his lips curling. "Everyone's had that whore."

Unlike me, he couldn't keep his voice down. The word *whore* drew some attention—both Miss Jennifer and Malachi frowned at us as they chatted with other kids close by.

Chuckling, I elbowed Chris. "Heard she smells like day-old tuna left out in the sun."

He burst out in laughter, and Malachi's scowl deepened.

"Let's get settled," our leader stated, his voice stern as he glanced around the circle of teens and sat into the chair beside Miss Jennifer. "Quiet down and open with prayer."

"I'd rather have a handful of tits and worship a

woman's pussy," I whispered so only my two buddies beside me would hear.

Chris barked out another laugh, and I bit against my own laughter wanting to burst out, my arms crossing as I slouched in my chair.

Malachi eyed the three of us, and I held his stare with a blatant one of my own. Lips pursed, he lowered his head, the rest of the group honoring his call to order.

I studied the wavy blond hair atop his down-turned head while he prayed God's blessing on our gathering, wondering if the strands would feel as silky between my itching fingertips as they appeared.

He said a hearty *amen*, and I leaned toward Chris, whispering truth out of the side of my mouth, "Worshiping *ass* would be even better."

"Hell yeah," he whispered back, shifting and chuckling.

Malachi glanced at us again.

Talk about a fucking power trip. Simply acting out gained me attention in the best way—his intense blue-eyed stare. Even disapproving, his rigid looks heated my blood. Thickened my dick.

I adjusted myself while he watched, a smirk on my face.

His gaze shot away, red creeping up his neck while he quoted scripture about unconditional love and acceptance, the same lesson he'd been teaching in Bible class for two weeks.

Fuck, what a trip.

Malachi tried, oh, how he tried to ignore me while in our circle of sheep-like teens, but whatever it was between us kept him coming back for more after he watched me adjust my junk.

The next time our eyes met, I touched the tip of my tongue to my lower lip.

Sucked it into my mouth the second time he looked my way.

He shifted too, sitting forward with elbows on his knees while talking to the group about showing kindness to our peers. Revealing God's love to all mankind even if we didn't agree with their religion or lifestyle.

Awesome lessons, just not ones usually followed by the Christians I'd known in my seventeen years.

"We can love the sinner without loving the sin," he stated, drawing more than one bob of head in agreement from kids who'd had the same teaching bashed into their heads since childhood. "Didn't Jesus sit and dine with Zacchaeus? Didn't he tell those wanting to judge the woman who'd committed adultery to cast the first stone only if they were without sin?"

He listed a few other times the God of the New Testament showed love when He could have condemned souls.

But Malachi didn't come right out and state that homosexuality was a sin—or bring up any of the others actually listed in the Bible. He didn't mention fire and brimstone or burning for eternity if one gave into the sins of the flesh like Dad preached at least once a month ever since that girl in high school got pregnant out of wedlock thanks to Chris's dick.

She'd gone to live with her grandparents, gave the kid up for adoption, and never came back to Elkin's Bible Church. She'd been quietly shunned, spoken of by Dad with his deacons and elders over the phone when he didn't know I listened in. But with Chris being an elder's son, he got off with a public repentance one Sunday morning after service.

Dad was judgmental as fuck, looking down his damn nose at those who fell, and if Chris had never repented, I'd have been forced to give up one of my few friends.

And Dad would behave the same and require the same if the truth about me ever came out.

A couple months until freedom...

But in the meantime, I kept on with my snide comments, riling the non-Christian school guys up until our whispers and laughter disrupted our youth group and drew attention like I'd wanted it to.

"If you boys don't quiet down," Malachi stated, "I'm going to have to separate you."

"What are we?" I muttered under my breath to Tyler on my left. "First graders?"

"Do you have words you wish to share with the rest of the group, Isaac?" Malachi called me out.

Arms crossed, I held his gaze. "Nope."

"You sure about that?" He surprised me by pushing. "Because it seems you've got something on your mind."

Oh, the things in my head. How would the so-called pious youth pastor behave if I told his youth group exactly what I thought about him and the lust I clearly saw in his gaze every time our eyes met?

My lazy grin hardened his countenance, and he looked away, changing the subject back to the lecture I expected he believed God had given him for the night.

Chris elbowed me, chuckling. Guess I'd earned his admiration, not that I cared.

Malachi's teaching veered into the importance of honesty. The fucking liar thought he could preach to the damn choir.

My first snort earned me a glare.

The second caused Miss Jennifer to shift in her seat beside him, her glance flickering between us. Malachi had to do something, and my stomach fluttered in anticipation. I imagined him dragging me out into the hallway. Slamming me into the wall and getting all up in my face.

Anger, an exchange of heated words—hell, maybe even heated touches.

Damn.

Another adjustment of my dick drew his focus.

He wrapped up his little lesson early, and the kids meandered into the usual social groups to play board games.

I stayed put, eyeing the youth pastor. Wondering and waiting as Chris and Tyler ambled away toward the senior girls.

Malachi and Miss Jennifer spoke quietly, and he glanced my way.

Come on, pastor man. Bring whatever discipline you want. I'm game.

I raised an eyebrow. Waited.

Lips pursed, his chest rose and fell like he took a fortifying breath—and he stood, walking toward me with sure, measured steps.

Fuck yes.

He took the empty seat beside me.

So much for those thoughts of being dragged into the hallway and pushed up against the wall.

"Are you okay, Isaac?"

I sucked in a lungful of his scent—dryer sheets and subtle aftershave. Damn delicious. Made my jeans strangle my dick. "Why wouldn't I be?"

"You seem...off tonight. Troubled."

"Troubled." I huffed a sarcastic laugh. "Sounds like you've been talking to my dad."

"I'm here to help, not judge."

I met Malachi's gaze, loving how an undercurrent of energy seemed to zap back and forth between us. Sitting that close, I noticed a few freckles on his nose. The perfect arch in his thinner upper lip. The pink in his plump lower one.

Not quite pouty but lickable all the same.

"Don't."

His one word jerked my focus off his mouth. "Don't what?"

"Look at me like that," he half-hissed, glancing around to see who might be watching our discussion.

"Like what?" I pushed, my pulse thrumming, my eyes narrowing.

He turned his attention back on my face. Held my stare until I felt lightheaded with need for something...*more.*

"I think you know what," Malachi stated sternly as though unaffected by our mutual attraction, "and it has to stop."

I pinched my bottom lip between two fingers, snagging his focus, my mouth curling at the butterflies wreaking havoc on my insides. "I like this."

"This?" he asked, his voice raspy and sexy as fuck.

"Us," I whispered, leaning forward slightly into his personal space.

"There is no us," Malachi snipped. "There never will be an us, and I would appreciate it if you would behave."

"But behaving is so...*boring.*"

A muscle ticked in his jaw, and I wondered what words he wanted to spew at me but felt as God's man he couldn't. "Don't push me, Isaac."

"Or what?"

Heat flared in his eyes, the kind that sent an ache through my groin and smeared pre-cum in my boxers. "Or I'll have a little talk to your father. Tell him why you act out."

"And why is that, *Malachi*?"

Fuck, he liked his name on my lips. His pupils swelled, and he leaned even closer, stealing my breath and stalling out my heartbeat. "To hide who you are inside."

Our gazes remained locked for a moment longer before he walked away without another word. I stared after him, processing, my held exhale leaving in a rush.

Who you are, he'd said, not what I *chose* to be, like Dad preached about my particular "sin."

My truth.

Malachi didn't believe homosexuality was a choice. Wondering what had led him to such a place solidified my thoughts on the man clear as hell in my head.

We were the same. We definitely *wanted* the same.

He'd tried to redirect my pursuit for attention, and he'd done nothing but double my craving for another verbal sparring match—and possibly more.

So, *so* much more.

9

———

MALACHI

Days passed. A full week, and another.

Isaac continued to test me, his vocal rebellion growing with every passing minute in his presence. I should've hated how he made me feel, the energy I fed off of, the *life* he swelled inside my chest.

He became the only person I could breathe freely around, and I didn't understand why, considering how the lust in his eyes caused my lungs to seize.

While he tempted my flesh and called to a libido left to rot where it belonged, I couldn't help the fact I came alive around him. Suppressing my desire for the young man didn't lessen the draw.

The craving for him.

Isaac was desperate for attention, same as I'd been as a kid. Pastor Bram, I came to realize within a matter of weeks, lived for his church. It was all he spoke about—his flock, his aspirations. Rarely did he mention his only son or any pride he felt in being a father.

The only time Pastor Bram talked about Isaac was when spouting off disappointments and negativity. His son had been the blessing he and Annabelle had prayed for, but the man took no joy in Isaac like my dad had done with me, especially when I'd approached him about Isaac failing Bible class.

The truth of his father, the exact opposite of my loving parents, expanded my empathy for Isaac, and I couldn't help but take it easy on him, regardless of how he got the boys in youth group going or how he shot me knowing looks that stiffened my dick to the point of pain.

I gave into the need for release and emptied my balls every day before leaving for the school or church. All in hopes that by sating my lust of the flesh, the appearance of Isaac wouldn't cause sinful imaginings since my prayers went unanswered.

But every glimpse of him, whether in the school's uniform blue slacks or ripped jeans on Wednesday nights youth group, cast my mind into depraved unholiness. Harmful thoughts, the type that God would punish me for if I didn't atone.

I couldn't talk to my pastor—hell no.

So I called the only man I could. As a Christian

counselor, I knew he would give me nonjudgmental truth.

"I'm on the cusp, Zeke."

"Talk to me."

I pinched the bridge of my nose, my head tipped against the back of my couch and my eyes clenched shut. We hadn't spoken in the three weeks since I'd arrived in Elkins, but I'd reached a breaking point. "Coming here was a mistake."

"Isaac is proving too much a temptation?"

"It's a strong draw between us, ten times more than I'd felt with Brian...it can't be ignored. I feel like I'm drowning in need."

"The lusts of the flesh."

I wanted to agree with the words Zeke spoke, but I couldn't. "It's more than mere lust," I admitted, letting out a heavy sigh, my free hand falling to the couch beside me. I saw Isaac in my mind's eye. His flashing hazel orbs and the smirk I wanted to bite off his lips. The hurt I sometimes caught when he glanced at me, the connection of...loneliness I felt radiating off him.

"It's more than lust," I reiterated, sitting forward to rest my elbows on my knees.

"More how?"

"I—I don't know." I huffed an exhale, hating how my stomach churned. "I want to protect him, to keep him from experiencing the same hurt I did."

"What do you mean?" Zeke sounded relaxed,

settled in for a long ass talk.

"He's a singer/songwriter." My throat tightened.

"Fuck."

"Yeah." My eyelids slid shut, my head hanging between my shoulders. "He's headed to Nashville after graduation, and the thought of what he'll face there, the temptation and evil... I can't allow that to happen."

"He needs to live his own life, Malachi. Make his own decisions, learn from his own mistakes."

"And end up in the same hole I barely managed to crawl out of?" I shot back, a spark of anger in my chest giving me something solid to hold onto.

"God pulled you from your depression."

"Did He?" I asked, truly wondering for the first time. "Because it sure as hell felt a lot like me dragging my own ass out. There was no angel's trumpet, no sense of heavenly arms wrapping my heavy heart up and carrying me to contentment. It was my decision to return to the Lord as Mom lay on her deathbed.

"Are you happy?"

Zeke's question caught me off guard, and I took time to consider what he asked.

True happiness came from the Lord and couldn't be manufactured by man, one's conscience, or another person in your life. However, I felt no such joy, no peace. I couldn't remember feeling that way since before Brian's car accident.

"No."

"I don't know what to say," Zeke murmured through my cell, and I swallowed hard. "I can only speak truth as I see it. God has a plan. He'll reveal himself in His time. You just have to trust Him until He does."

Trusting. Blind faith.

When what I longed for stood right in front of me.

"Can I pray with you?"

I didn't deny my best friend's need to offer comfort in the only way he could with being a few hours away. The words of thanks on my lips didn't resonate in my soul when he finished, nor did my vocalized appreciation when he promised to continue to pray for God to guide me.

Hanging up, I didn't feel any better than before I'd placed the call.

God still hid behind a shroud, but I began to wonder if the darkness closing over me was of my own making.

I fell to my knees, tears on my cheeks, begging forgiveness for my sinful thoughts, for my wandering mind.

No sense of calmness swept in to smother my guilt in the hour I knelt before His throne.

And no joy promised in the Bible came in the morning either.

10

ISAAC

School sucked. Church sucked. Youth group made my gut clench to the point I felt like I was going to puke every time I entered the gymnasium and found the usual circle of folding chairs.

Like a damn accountability group...

I glanced around the echoing room, arms crossed and offering glares for each and every one of the idiots around me. Behaving like a brat came easily, stemming from bottled up anger. I wanted to lash out. To barrel through anyone who stood in my way.

I needed to escape.

"Hey." Miss Jennifer's light hold on my arm drew my focus off of Malachi chatting with a few of the younger kids over near the games table.

"Hey." I gave her my full attention, an impulsive

decision slamming into my brain. "I want to do that demo for your cousin."

She bit her lip, glancing across the gymnasium. "About that..."

"What?" She'd been so damn on board, pushing for so long, and now she hesitated?

"Malachi said your dad wouldn't approve."

"My dad." I clenched my jaw, catching the youth pastor's gaze across the spacious room that echoed with laughter, something I hadn't felt in too long.

"I know your father has high hopes for you, Isaac. Bible college...maybe seminary."

My dad wanted me to follow in his footsteps, but if he had any inkling of my inner workings, he would never suggest such a thing.

If anyone, Malachi would understand my urge to get away—far away—and make my own decisions. Stating my father knew best...

Heat roused inside me, and not the kind that tempted me to attack him in some dark hallway with grasping hands and searching lips.

"Whatever." I pulled free from her hold and found a chair. I slouched there, arms crossing once more, my stare on my sneakers.

Chris threw himself into the chair beside me, filling me in on his latest conquest—some college chick home for the summer already. Blow jobs, hands jobs...I barely heard a word he said with how my mind churned over the youth pastor's audacity to attempt directing my future.

Although hot as fuck, he'd landed on my shit list again.

Malachi called our little meeting to order while I wondered why the fuck I sat in a circle of teens I didn't have a goddamn thing in common with. Not one.

They wanted to worship a God I didn't truly believe in. Sing his praises while I stayed silent. Malachi's husky tenor united in perfect harmony with Miss Jennifer's as they led us in songs.

Closing my eyes, I drowned in his voice. Focused on it amidst the sea of off-tune girls and the one teenage guy in our group who thought he could sing.

I hummed a weaving harmony around Malachi's in my head, taking the alto when he stayed on tenor, seamlessly switching parts as the music led him. The beauty we created—fuck, it made me hard. Got my blood rushing full of adrenaline and a high I could ride for eternity.

He and I would blend like fucking perfection in real life—I didn't have a doubt. But I refused to sing praises in church.

And Malachi wanted to stomp on my dreams.

I attempted to squash down the brew of hope inside me, facing reality. Malachi going the Q&A route that night, drawing in the teens for conversation about God's word, their beliefs, and their convictions, made it easier. I scuffed my toes against the gymnasium floor, only half listening, just waiting for the night to be over already.

"It's just so wrong, you know?" The girl beside me stated and let out a sigh, her voice trembling enough that I paid attention.

"If there's a heartbeat," one of the boys said, "it's murder. Plain and simple."

I glanced up at the boy—one of the deacon's sons. Dogmatic as fuck, a self-righteous tenth grader who probably hadn't realized he could do more with his dick than take a piss.

"Abortion has been fought over in the courts when it has to do with God's word, not the law." That last statement from a girl too young to know her pussy from her ass caused my brow to furrow.

"So you're suggesting a woman's womb is nothing but an incubator?" I shot back, earning me her wide-eyed stare. "You think a woman shouldn't have a say over what she can and can't do with her own body?" I huffed a snort. "What happens when you get kidnapped off the street one day while walking home from school?"

"Isaac."

I ignored Malachi, my gaze plastered on the young girl. "What happens when he rapes you?"

"Isaac!" Jennifer gasped.

"And you end up pregnant," I continue, ignoring the shifting and murmurs around me. "What do you do then? Thank God for the life growing inside you fathered by a sick rapist?" I snipped, my blood pressure rising. "You don't think you should have the choice whether you raise the life or end the pregnancy before it even begins?"

One of the deacon's sons jumped in. "There's a heartbeat at—"

"I don't give a flying fuck when the heart first beats."

"Isaac!" Malachi stood in my periphery, but I kept my glare on the kid who spouted bullshit at me.

"You believe a woman should be forced to carry around a pile of cells and be thankful for nine months of hell after suffering rape? What the hell is wrong with you?"

A hand closed over my arm, yanking me to my feet. "Let's go."

I stumbled along behind Malachi out into the hallway, my dick swelling to life at the firm hold he had on my bare arm.

Skin on skin.

First contact since our handshake weeks ago.

His touch seared me, and goosebumps skittered across my neck. Took my dick to full mast in three quick breaths.

He slammed open the janitor's closet, shoved me in, and flicked on the lights. "You've been asking for it all night."

Malachi had no fucking clue what I really

wanted to ask for, what had me pissed off at the world. The heat, the energy boiling up between us, took me to the edge of reason.

"The fuck is *your* problem?" I half hollered, shoving against his hard chest. Lusting for more. So much more. "You come in here all high and mighty, thinking you're God's man—"

He growled, grasped my neck, and slammed me into the wall.

Fuck yes.

Heat exploded throughout my body, and I gasped, needing him to fall over with me, to lose himself in whatever it was that boiled like lava between us.

"I see the way you look at me," I spat, glaring and ready to punch or bite his face. I couldn't decide which I desired more. I settled for grabbing his wrist as he held me in place.

"How do I look at you?" His voice quivered, his eyes half wild. Pupils blown wide.

So goddamn hot I wanted to sink my teeth into his lower lip.

"Like you'd love nothing more than to bend me over the nearest desk, pew, or chair, and fuck the brat right out of me."

A shudder rippled over him, but he didn't speak. Didn't deny what I'd bet my life was true.

I snorted, lifting my chin even higher, submitting my neck to his hand. "You think you know me.

Think you can work alongside my dad to keep me bound in these chains when all I want is to breathe free? I'm going to Nashville the day I turn eighteen, and I don't give a flying fuck—"

"No."

The fucker had balls. "I heard what you told Miss Jennifer. Who the *fuck* do you think you are to rain on my damn parade?"

"Someone who's lived it. Failed at it. *Hurt* for it." Pain filled his voice, his eyes, but I wasn't about to soften for his ass when he still held me tight against the wall.

"So?" I shot back.

Malachi closed the distance between us. Clothing separated our skin, but I could feel the hard length of him, the muscle, the bone. A body I wanted to fall to my knees and worship.

Pure agony overflowed from his blue eyes, damn near stabbing me in the heart. "I can't bear the thought of you feeling what I did. The mistakes I made..."

Oh no, he wasn't going to trail off and leave me hanging. I wanted his secrets. Needed to hear why he buried who he was deep inside, refusing to let himself live. "Tell me."

Malachi stilled, his whole body seeming to buzz with an energy that reached through my clothing to whisper against my skin, lighting every cell inside me on fire. "I can't, he whispered, but he didn't release his hold on my neck as his gaze slid down to my mouth.

I swallowed, knowing something deep rooted inside him, issues he wouldn't uncover no matter how much I begged. But he didn't have to speak them. "So show me," I rasped out, shifting so our dicks rubbed against each other, lighting fire in my veins.

"Isaac."

My heart fluttered crazily in my chest. "I want it, Malachi."

He groaned and took my mouth with bruising force. Lips, teeth, tongue—my first kiss. He sucked the oxygen from my lungs and dizzied my brain with every hungry groan escaping him.

Affirmation.

Pleasure I hadn't expected from a simple act.

Malachi owned me without speaking a word. The firmness of his lips and the hint of coffee and wintergreen on his breath as he licked at my mouth damn near brought me to the ground.

If he commanded me to get on my knees, I would willingly go.

If he'd ordered me to turn and bend over to let him fuck me without a damn drop of lube, I'd have gladly done so.

He devoured me, ate at my mouth like a man starved for salvation, a soul surrounded by a sea of hopelessness, floundering.

Lost.

In need of saving.

Same as the deepest parts of me. I wanted him to know I understood—that I needed the same thing as him.

I reached between us and grabbed hold of his length through his slacks. Malachi's dick was bigger than mine. Thicker. A shudder wracked through me as I imagined him shoving his length into my body, claiming and taking what we both craved.

"Malachi," I whimpered as his lips and teeth trailed along my jawline, his grasp on my neck tightening as he thrust into my hand's hold again and again. "Fuck..." I swallowed, his palm closed over my throat making it damn near impossible.

He shuddered and breathed hard, resting his forehead against mine, the bulk of him still holding me against the wall. "This is wrong."

The rasp in his voice caused precum to ooze from my dick, and I ground my groin against the back of my hand working him over his pants.

"Stop." He grabbed my wrist to stop me from tempting him for more. "Please, Isaac...I—I can't do this."

"We already are."

"We can't." He stepped back, his eyebrows furrowed and eyes darkened by lust yet full of guilt. Fists at his sides and his entire body trembling, he stared at me.

I gasped for breath. Hoped my neck would bruise so I'd have something to remember my first kiss by.

"I made so many wrong choices, Isaac." Malachi shook his head as though trying to rid his mind of the past. "I would do anything to keep you from the same. And this...this is definitely a mistake that would lead to something I can't be responsible for."

"I'm going to pursue my dream," I stated with a shaky voice, refusing to be commanded by yet another man who thought himself in a position of authority over me.

A muscle ticked in his jaw, but he didn't make a move to touch me again like the energy between us demanded.

I couldn't bear the idea of rejection—so I left on shaky legs. Walked around him and out of the closet without another word, without a backward glance even though my heart longed for both.

Our time together grew shorter and shorter.

But I wasn't done with Malachi Foley.

A combustion awaited us, I didn't doubt, but the timing, the when and how...

We just needed a few moments away from the church, away from a place that would remind him of his job, my age, my parentage.

Maine, I promised.

11

MALACHI

The door slammed shut behind Isaac, and I leaned my forehead against it. His flavor lingered on my lips, and I found myself licking them, hoping for another hint of cinnamon. Spicy and sweet—a damn addiction I'd gotten a taste of and feared I wouldn't ever rid my mind from its draw.

Addiction.

Of the worst sort, the sinful kind, of which action would damn us to eternal hell, same as it had done to Brian.

"I won't allow it," I whispered into the janitor closet's ear-ringing stillness. Sucking in a lungful of chemical-laced air, I fought against the throb in my dick, the tightness in my groin. "I won't lead him into temptation like I did with Brian."

An ache replaced the hollowness in my chest,

and I rubbed at my shirt, hating it more than emptiness.

Speaking the truth I wanted wouldn't make it come to pass, no matter how much the Bible promised.

Just a few weeks left to the school year—and then I would only have to put up with his rebellious ass on Wednesday nights rather than every day. But if I was being honest with myself, I would miss the ebb and flow of teasing and annoyance that had led to the most heated kiss of my life.

My lips continued to tingle, my fingertips still throbbing in time with the pulse I'd felt strumming like hell beneath them when I'd held Isaac by his neck.

I didn't doubt I'd taken his first kiss. I'd caught him off guard, but he'd overcome his surprise, giving back in the same way I'd lusted for with unpracticed lips. Uninhibited, he'd been handsy and greedy for more.

Fuck, what a temptation he was.

Standing, I filled my lungs and squeezed the base of my dick rather than jerking off like I wanted to do.

Seventeen.

Pastor's son.

Male—the biggest forbidden element as far as my station was concerned.

But I told myself all I wanted to think on was

saving him from himself, from heading off into the unknown as a naive young man dozens would prey on given the chance. I couldn't allow it. Wouldn't. I had to find a way to save him from the life I'd lived.

———

I managed a few prayers in the following weeks while counting down the days until classes let out for the summer. Begging God for strength, for His mercy—but I couldn't find it in myself to ask forgiveness for putting my hands on Isaac. Dominating him with a mere hold on his neck, fucking into his fumbling grasp on my dick.

Jerking off to the memory became my favorite pastime, and as every day passed, my guilt over doing so lessened more and more.

I grew numb to the sin of taking myself in hand and fantasizing about a teenage boy. My body's craving for him couldn't be sated.

At least I made the right decisions whenever in his presence. I ignored him and pretended the energy he brought to my existence wasn't real.

It was for the best, even though it killed me inside. Sticking to what was proper leader-wise, I shared passages of scripture that spoke of choosing a holy life, making right decisions and forgiving ourselves if we failed, trusting God's plan—his path.

All of which I didn't, couldn't, do.

Maybe if Isaac heard the words of grace and mercy enough, he'd reconsider when faced with choices that could lead to devastation.

On graduation night, I sat in the church's auditorium, clapping with pride for each and every kid who walked up in their blue robes and caps with happiness on their faces.

Alphabetically, that left Isaac last to cross the stage, but the smirk on his face wasn't one of joy—it was full of mischief, a glint of rebellion that promised he'd be gone from my life soon.

The substance his presence always brought to my chest faded as I considered him truly leaving.

I knew he wouldn't stick around Elkins.

Nashville hadn't ever been spoken of again, but he'd made his dreams clear, and his dad grumbled about Isaac stating he wanted to take a year off before heading to Bible college.

Isaac had no such intention of following in Pastor Bram's footsteps, I didn't doubt that one bit. He would choose the way he wanted, religion, his parents, and the church be damned.

And I would be left behind where I belonged, once more struggling to breathe, having nightmares about what choices he faced every day without guidance.

I just hoped the words I'd shared through the weeks would help keep him in truth. Keep his mind, body, and soul safe.

Isaac's focus flitted over the congregation as he crossed the stage, his gaze landing on me for a brief moment. I allowed him to hold me enthralled, the touch of his tongue to his lower lip tightening my groin and making me rub over my pectorals.

I want you.

Crave you.

You're my worst temptation and the air in my lungs.

I tore my focus off him and smiled at Annabelle beside me, the joy on her face making me wonder if she might choose to love her son once she and her husband learned the truth of who he was.

Not my circus, I told myself, glancing over the rest of the graduates as they tossed their caps into the air. *And definitely not my monkey.*

12

ISAAC

Almost free...almost free...

I chanted my new favorite saying in my head while watching the backs of Malachi's and Miss Jennifer's heads in the bus's front seat. We ended up hiring an actual full-sized bus and driver for our trip to Maine since so many of the teens in youth group had signed up.

Kids chatted around me, and some played road games, their laughter nothing but a buzz in my ears.

Tyler hadn't been able to make the trip—summer soccer or some such shit—so Chris ended up being my seat partner, my only friend in our group. Not that he knew a damn thing about the real me though.

Miss Jennifer leaned close to Malachi, her bright smile in profile, and he smiled at whatever she said to him.

I stewed on my plastic seat that squeaked every time I moved, the material sticking to the backs of my thighs since I'd been an idiot, and I'd worn shorts rather than jeans like I usually did.

Almost eight hours in and I'd had about enough of the noise and enough of the BO from the beefy guy beside me. The singing encouraged by Miss Jennifer who stared at Malachi with stars in her eyes made my skin crawl.

Did he even realize she had a thing for him? Did he understand that continuing to be friendly, to laugh and listen, encouraged her? His gay ass obviously had no fucking clue—or was he forcing himself into a role that was expected by good little Christians? Did he want to choose a woman so that everyone around him wouldn't know about his "sin?"

Did he want to be so-called normal in the eyes of man?

As though hearing my thoughts, he glanced over his shoulder, our gazes connecting.

Clashing with a flow of energy, of lust and longing that chubbed my dick.

We hadn't spoken a word to each other in private since that moment in the janitor's closet. Not since the day he'd blown my world to bits and gave my mind the best fuel to fantasize over.

I remembered the feel of his mouth, the hunger

of his groans, and the hardness of his dick in my hand.

I wanted that dick.

In my mouth. In my ass.

I just lusted after Malachi Foley in every sense of the word, and sin and parents could go straight the fuck to hell as far as I was concerned.

And a five-day trip awaited us, one without Dad and Mom, one with an authority figure I knew how to wear down.

My A-game lay in wait.

Naughty as fuck, my mind had conjured up some good shit to break him down. I wanted him putty in my hands—and I needed his hands on me. Wrecking me. Breaking me. Putting me back together again.

Whatever it was that connected us, that made me aware every time he drew within a few feet's distance of me, it was potent. The kind of drug that swirled my head in what I expected drunkenness or being high must feel like.

His face remained passive as we stared at one another. His eyes were empty of emotion, lips void of the parted inhales of passion even as the memory stiffened my cock while sitting on a damn bus surrounded by innocence.

I pursed my lips in a slight, mocking kiss he wouldn't be able to misinterpret.

Malachi turned back around, his countenance impressively unmoved.

Fucking liar.

Smirking, I studied the back of his head.

Soon, my dear youth pastor. Soon.

"Did Tyler tell you I asked Sara out?"

I shook my head at Chris's question, glancing at the girl he spoke of on the other side of the aisle and up two rows.

Short blonde to his dark mass. Day and night. I couldn't imagine how their hooking up could be accomplished considering their height difference. Not that I wanted the visual.

"She's on the no-touch love train," I told him, casting him a sideways glance.

He stared at her like I did Malachi, but the bone-head obviously hadn't noticed my actions the way I did his.

"She's got curves for days," he said, still staring. "Those tits would fill even my hands." He held up said massive hands, turning them with his fingers spread, as though grasping her breasts.

"Great rack," I agreed without a bit of truth behind my statement.

"I'd like her on her knees," he mumbled even though the teens on the seats around us couldn't hear in the ruckus of the bus. "Holding those tits together, letting me fuck them. I'd blow my load all over her skin."

Any normal guy's dick would get a rise out of that idea, so I played along. "Can I watch?"

He chuckled and elbowed me. "Sick fuck."

"Voyeur at heart," I lied some more. "So, what's your plan?"

"Get her to take a little walk with me one night instead of singing Kumbaya around the campfire."

Fucking awesome idea, a definite way to get someone alone.

I eyed the back of Malachi's head again as Chris laid out his thoughts on how to get a taste of Sara. Eventually talk her into fucking because that was one pussy he wanted to own.

"Let me know if you need any help in making that fantasy come true," I told him, my own mind considering how to get our youth pastor all to myself again.

Somehow, someway...

Not soon enough.

We finally pulled into the youth hostel before I figured out a clear plan of how to do more than wear him down. A sprawling disjointed motel-ish building, the likes of which I'd never seen outside of Maine, sat in the downpour that had pounded the bus's roof the last few miles while driving through the woods.

A barn connected to the garage, connected to a mudroom of sorts, connected to a laundry room, connected to an old eighteenth century house, connected to an eighties "modern" home. The last was two floors, the second of which housed the large rooms all the teens would bunk in.

I followed on Malachi's heels as our host led us up the stairs I'd climbed three times before in my high school years. He sat his bag on the lower bunk beside the door like our old youth pastor always used to do—I put mine on the next bed rather than as deep into the room as I usually did, sliding my guitar case beneath.

He didn't look my way and didn't acknowledge my presence, but I saw the stiffness of his shoulders as I claimed the bed closest to where he would lay at night.

Hopefully in nothing but boxers. Naked would be even better.

"Don't worry," I murmured, walking past him and out the door. "I don't snore."

He shivered. Full on body ripple that caused excitement to swell in my veins and puff my chest.

Chuckling, I made my way downstairs, shoulders back, chin tilted up with an arrogance that Malachi himself had brought on even though I'd never lacked in the self-confidence area. While I wasn't ripped like a body builder and didn't pack bulk onto my medium frame, I didn't have an ounce of fat on my body. Lean swimmer's muscle covered my bones from countless hours swimming and mowing lawns, and I took pride in keeping them defined.

Considering how I'd caught Malachi checking me out when he didn't think anyone looked, I knew he liked what he saw. Made me want to preen like a damn peacock. Stick out my ass a bit more than usual, maybe even add a sway to my hips.

Every one of the teens drew straws, and I ended up on dinner duty, helping the older couple hosting our group to get food on the table. Spaghetti with sauce from a jar, iceberg lettuce chopped up with ranch dressing. Loaves of generic white sandwich bread with buttery spread from a tub.

Nothing like Mom's home-cooked meals, but everyone ate without complaint.

At least the church taught good manners in honoring their elders.

I had zero intentions of honoring jack shit when it came to Malachi though. I would serve like we'd gone to Maine to do. I would labor outside in the garden and flower beds that choked with weeds. I would help rebuild the rock wall falling down on the eastern section of the property closer to the Appalachian Trail.

But I would find a way to wreck him.

He had said that day in the janitor closet that we *couldn't*...that there was no *us*. Well, he didn't know the level of determination I had residing deep inside me. My desire to know him, to sin with him, would damn our souls to hell for eternity if one believed in such a thing.

Even if he was like Dad with his holier than thou shit, I didn't care. He looked too damn good in a pair of low-riding jeans and tight T-shirt to be ignored.

Especially once said shirt grew dark with sweat and smeared with mud the next day.

I stared more than I ought to while he lugged rocks around with Chris, sweat beading on his brow, dripping down his cheek. Forearms flexing, veins popping along his tree tattoo that led up to tribal ones on his upper arm I wanted to trace with my tongue. Moving rocks alongside him, Chris, and a few other guys didn't come easy while dealing with a semi all afternoon.

And too bad the showers weren't an open concept in the gym like at the public school. Two separate stalls with curtains...but I made sure to head to the bathroom at the same time Malachi did after we finished our labor of love for the day.

I hadn't gotten a peek when he'd shimmied out of his boxer briefs—beneath the towel wrapped tightly around his trim waist. But at least I'd had a few seconds to check out his ass in the cotton clinging to his backside.

My youth pastor was sex on a stick while moving into the adjoining men's bathroom, a tease of the worst proportions, and holy hell did I drool. At least on the guy's side of the second floor and bathroom, no Miss Jennifer stood around to enjoy an eyeful of his golden, tanned skin like I managed to do.

I finally got to see Malachi's tribal-like tattoo on his upper arm that ran over to his shoulder. Bare, hairless chest with pecs I wanted to bite. Nipples that would look hot as fuck with rings pierced through them.

He didn't glance my way when I followed him into the bathroom and shut the door behind us. He didn't speak. Didn't turn.

My dick tented my towel, and the second he disappeared behind his chosen stall, towel flipping up and over the wall, I stepped into the one beside him. Hung my own towel, my pulse racing.

Grinning like a fool because I'd managed to beat Chris to the bathroom who'd grumbled about getting first dibs on the shower. He'd run into Sara who'd been working in the garden all day. She'd pulled him up short in the living room area on the first floor.

I turned on the blasting water and closed my eyes as it heated, listening to the spray from both shower heads and imagining Malachi washing his gorgeous body from neck to toes. My fingertips tingled with the wish to do it for him.

I soaped up every inch of my own skin, envisioning his hands smearing the suds, cupping my balls, and stroking my aching length. Lower lip between my teeth, I gave over to the fantasy whole-heartedly until my head tipped back, and I sucked oxygen through flared nostrils while fucking my hand.

The bathroom walls did nothing to muffle noise, and I knew if I groaned too loudly, other guys out in the bunk area outside might hear.

Couldn't have that, so I half-swallowed my moans, still audible enough to the one man in the bathroom with me.

Skin slapped, an unmistakable sound to any guy.

Whimpers rose from my chest as I fucked through my fist, fantasizing Malachi's hot breath brushed over my ear, his raspy voice telling me how much he wanted to watch his cum drip from my gaping hole.

"Fuck," I whispered—and spunk shot out of me, a boatload since I hadn't jacked off in two days.

Holy hell...

I lowered my head with a groan Malachi would hear and watched my hand milk myself dry, my ass clenching at emptiness I wanted him to fill with every thrust.

The clearing of a throat to my right made me grin as the last spurt dribbled from my slit, and my lips parted to suck down oxygen.

He'd definitely heard me.

I rinsed and shut off my water, my stomach light and my head giddy. Relief, even if not in the way I would have preferred, lessened the tension that had ridden me all day. I strained my ears to listen, wondering how Malachi's body reacted and if he would care for it the same way I had.

His shower still ran, the unmistakable sounds of schlicking—hand fucking—in my ears.

Fuck, yes.

My lingering semi twitched while my mouth watered, but I'd drained myself dry and wouldn't get it up again for at least fifteen minutes or so.

Rather than dry off in my stall, I stepped out into the bathroom, hoping for a peek around Malachi's curtain. The fantasy of seeing him jerk off was potent enough that I almost reached out and moved the damn barrier between us.

A quiet gasp from his shower stall picked my pulse back up, and I swallowed hard. "Need any help?" I asked quietly, unable to keep the smirk off my face as my insides buzzed.

Malachi let out a curse—a grunt—and the slick sounds of a fist fuck ended.

Shit...holy fucking hell, he did it.

Did he watch himself empty like I had? Lips parted while panting quietly, wishing it was me who'd been the one touching him?

I hoped it was my ass, my mouth, he imagined while getting himself off. Even better, I wanted my body doing the work for him.

Cursing in my head and shaking from the adrenaline rush over what we'd done, I toweled myself dry.

His shower shut off, his towel hanging over the wall yanked from sight.

I rubbed mine against my hair, eyes on his barrier, waiting for it to move.

Head down, he slid the curtain aside. Water droplets still clung to his chest and dripped from his hair. The towel wrapped snug around his waist, but the sight of his lower abs and that sinful V and light-haired happy trail disappearing beneath cotton readied my dick for action even though I thought I'd need longer to recoup.

Enough sexual tension clung in the humid air between us that I didn't need to speak. Breathing heavily, I turned sideways, giving him the opportunity to glance my way if he wanted—and he did.

Right at my swelling dick. It jumped beneath his heated stare while I toweled at my hair again, my heart racing.

Turning, I gave him a full view.

He jerked his head away from me faster than a serpent's strike.

Lower lip between my teeth again, I dried off my sack, my dick bobbing.

He side-eyed me, so I repeated the action.

"Isaac," he croaked out my name, and I grinned.

"Yeah?" I rasped out a reply, my hands falling to my sides, the towel at my left.

Lips pursed, he shook his head—and stalked out

of the bathroom, leaving me alone with my hard dick and a big ass grin on my face.

My youth pastor wanted me. Badly.

And it was only a matter of time before he gave in to what he considered temptation—what I knew would be heaven on earth.

13

MALACHI

Every time I turned around, either Jennifer or Isaac was up my butt. The thought of taking a *dick* up my ass hadn't interested me since that first time with Elliot, Jennifer's cousin.

But Isaac? He made me lust for things I never thought I would again, most of all, the chance to bottom.

There wasn't anything I didn't want with him. Hearing him jerk off in the shower beside mine lessened my willpower to say no.

Other teens had been in our bunk room when we'd wrapped towels around our waists and dropped our drawers beneath. He'd followed on my heels like he'd done all day, and it would have drawn more attention for me to tell him to shower later, after me, when there were two stalls in the guys' bathroom.

The thought of being alone with him in that small bathroom had me half-hard before I yanked the shower curtain closed behind me, and being the brat Isaac was, he didn't bother keeping quiet while jerking off.

My ears strained as I washed, catching the quiet gasp, a slight moan. I fisted myself without thought, slowly riding along with him, wishing for an alternate reality where I could lock the bathroom door and push aside his curtain.

Watch as he fucked his own hand.

Press his chest against the shower wall and grasp his chin to hold his head to the side so I could devour his mouth while I took over and fucked the ass he liked to stick out and tease me with.

Eyes clenched shut, hand working regardless of the prickling guilt in the back of my head, I soaked in every muffled noise from him, the echo of spraying water nearly drowning out the sexy as hell whimpers I could hear passing those pouty lips.

He cursed, and I bit back a groan, knowing he came.

I cleared my throat on a near cough to show my disapproval, but I couldn't help the need coursing through me.

Panting, I tilted my head back, hips meeting my downward strokes...faster. Harder.

Isaac's shower cut off, the squeak of curtain rings over metal letting me know he stood a thin plastic material away. Did he stare at my shower stall, wondering what I did? He had to hear it at least, since I damn near strangled my dick.

Fuck.

Unable to help myself, I faced the curtain, watching it through rising steam from the hot water pounding my aching shoulders. I imagined Isaac's focus on me, my tightened abs rippling as I fucked my hand, envisioning it was his tight hole squeezing the life out of my length.

A gasp flew from my parted lips as tingles raced up through my balls.

"Need any help?"

I imagined him bent over, my hands holding his cheeks apart...on his knees, mouth wide open and wanting, his mischievous eyes focused upward on my face.

Oh fuck.

My balls erupted, and I grunted my release regardless of the fact he knew what I did hidden from the world like I was.

Fucking brat. But what had I thought would happen when he followed me into the bathroom? I should have stopped it before it even started.

Jaw clenched and legs weak, I rinsed myself and shut off my shower. Quiet rang in my ears. I yanked my towel from the wall and did a half-dry, needing to get the hell out of that bathroom—far from sin incarnate.

Tucking my towel tight around my waist, I inhaled until it hurt. Threw open my curtain with my gaze on the floor, intent on escape.

My periphery showed he held his towel at his side. Dried off a bit and angled away, giving my frozen dumb ass a chance to look at his naked perfection. I took it in like Eve must have with that first juicy bite of forbidden fruit.

Isaac's dick stood upright, a good inch shorter than mine, but the girth made my asshole clench. His length pulsed beneath my stare, bumping against his tight lower belly.

He turned toward me, and I tore my focus from him, still unable to make my feet move. He dried off his balls in my periphery, and I gave him my full attention with a side-eye stare, uncaring that he knew I watched, unmoved as I was.

My hands clenched at my sides, my entire body vibrating with need—to attack him. Touch him. Kiss and bite his lips, take his dick in my hand and jerk us off together. Pick him up and order him to wrap his pale legs around my waist so my dick had access to his virgin ass.

Fuck, I wanted him to be a virgin. Mine.

"Isaac," I heard myself whisper his name like a prayer at the thought of sinking deep inside his hot body and owning the fuck out of him.

"Yeah?" He dropped his hands to his sides, not

covering his nakedness or making any attempts to ward me off or tell me no.

Fuck. Fucking hell...Christ.

Swallowing hard, I stalked away on reluctant feet, yanking the bathroom door open so hard in my attempt to escape temptation I was surprised the damn thing didn't rip from its hinges.

Isaac stayed shut up in the bathroom long enough that I had time to throw clothes over my damp body and get the hell downstairs to safety.

Jennifer sat in the living area at the bottom of the steps leading up to the boys' bunk room, obvious interest in her eyes as her gaze flicked over my wet head, my scruffy jaw, and down over my T-shirt. She looked away just as quickly before reaching my groin that wouldn't have tightened beneath her wandering eyes for anything.

Jaw still set, I settled in the recliner to her right, facing the stairs.

"You must be beat," she said with a smile in her voice like always. "You guys moved a ton of rocks today."

I grunted an affirmative. Lifting boulder-sized chunks of granite all day, the largest in the various piles due to Chris and me being the only big guys in our group, had done my muscles in. But exhaustion lay far from my mind.

"The weather will be perfect for a campfire tonight."

I grunted another affirmative.

"Usually the first evening is the best, the kids riding the high of being cooped up in the bus all day. Excitement and lots of praise and worship time."

It'd rained when we arrived at the hostel the night before, the rambunctious kids trapped in the room Jennifer and I sat in. A handful of other kids scattered around the room waiting for dinner, some playing board games and two reading in their own corners.

"I was thinking..." Jennifer's voice trailed off in my consciousness as the stairs creaked, and every single brain cell I had focused on who descended.

I recognized the ripped jeans and black Vans as they appeared, and my pulse picked up as Isaac stepped into sight.

He wore a dark green shirt that always made his eyes greener than hazel. Lower arms slightly sunburned since I hadn't allowed the guys to take their shirts off while laboring outside.

Paler neck. Pouty lips. Pink cheekbones that had also gotten too much sun. Eyes focused on mine, full of heat and intent. And his damn smirk. I lusted to hold him down and fuck it right out of him until he whimpered and cried for me to let him come.

Caught by the kid's stare, all I could do was breathe, my hands grasping the recliner's worn armrests.

Isaac reached the floor, the knowing in his eyes

like a punch to my gut. Our gazes glued as he ambled past, the set of his shoulders and the angle of his chin revealing a cockiness that intensified my desire to get a true taste of his sweet and spicy mouth.

I craved to have him boneless, sweat covered, and sated beneath me. Begging for me to stop because his ass had enough.

But I wanted to be wrecked by him too.

Refusing to turn my head to watch him pass into the kitchen area, I swallowed hard enough I coughed. My heart pounded in my chest, and I fought to focus on whatever Jennifer talked about. Something about two of our dating teens...she'd heard a rumor.

Her voice lowered, and I turned to face her fully, forcing myself to pay attention as the youth leader, the responsible one in charge of over a dozen teenagers.

"Sara's friend Marley told me she overheard her and Chris talking about sneaking away tonight."

That bit perked my ears up. That sounded like a damn good time if it were me and Isaac, but I frowned. "We'll need to keep an eye open."

Jennifer nodded, her gaze flitting over my face.

The light in her eyes made me uncomfortable as hell—like she imagined slinking off into the woods with me rather than sitting by the planned bonfire. She'd change her tune real quick if she knew who *I* wanted pressed up against a tree trunk.

Isaac moved around the dining area beyond Jennifer, helping our hosts prepare dinner even though he hadn't been on duty that evening. He smiled, carrying on a conversation with the elderly woman and carrying things to and from the table while Jennifer continued to chatter in my ear.

He placed napkins alongside each paper plate. Set out plasticware with precision, bending a few times to showcase his round ass in those jeans my fingers itched to rip from his body.

As though he could feel my stare, he glanced over his shoulder with hooded eyes and the damn smirk that plumped his lower lip.

Fuck.

Jaw once more clenching, I shifted my focus off him. If Isaac knew I watched him, others had to notice. None of the kids in the living room paid attention to me and Jennifer, I took note of while my gaze flitted around the spacious room.

"I think separating them would be best," Jennifer continued to speak, her countenance revealing nothing but attraction for me. Not even true concern for the two kids she discussed.

I agreed with her, deciding to stick close to Chris. The idea didn't turn me on, but knowing Isaac would be attached to him like he'd been since climbing on the bus definitely did.

At least if Isaac sat on Chris's other side, I wouldn't be faced with having him in direct line of sight. Less chance of my attention snagging on him —and getting caught by the others with sinful lust written across my face.

———

We started off the night with making s'mores, the kids all having to get their own sticks for roasting marshmallows. I stayed on Chris's heels as he and Isaac headed off with Sara and Marley in the direction of the woods, mere feet from the fire pit area.

The flames already reached upward into the sky as we burned old oak pallets, lighting the way toward the woods' edge.

Chris walked with Sara, leaning down to whisper in her ear. She giggled, glancing at Marley on her right.

Isaac slowed his step, bringing him alongside me. "Nice night."

I side eyed him, keeping my main focus on Chris and wondering what the hell the boys had up their sleeves.

"Kinda warm, though."

I grunted a noise he could take however he wanted.

"Gonna need another shower."

A flash of him with his head tipped back while

fisting his length made me stumble over a root as we stepped into the woods.

"I think I used up most of the hot water," Isaac continued with a conversational tone, "but beating off never felt so satisfying."

"What?" I turned, giving him my full attention, sure I hadn't heard him right.

He grinned at me, half of his face lit by the fire, the other half cast in darkness from the night. "I said, the hot water beating over me never felt so satisfying."

Had I been so damn caught up in the memory of listening to him earlier in the day that I'd misheard? Shaking my head, I lifted my focus to check out the closest tree. A few branches hung low, offering perfect marshmallow sticks.

I reached up, pulling one down.

Isaac stepped in close, keeping me distracted, the clean scent of his soap and cinnamon reaching me through the pine needles and leaf litter beneath our feet. Even the waft of woodsmoke from the fire couldn't erase him from my nose.

Drool coated my mouth at the memory of his taste. Sweet and innocent. Hungry and fumbling for more.

Definitely a virgin.

"Need any help?" he asked too damn close to my ear.

I scuttled sideways, focusing on stripping the

smaller twigs off the branch I'd ripped from the tree rather than how he made my groin ache. "I'm good."

"I'll bet you are," he murmured, heading back the way we'd come, swaying his ass enough that I knew he did so on purpose.

Damn brat.

Scowling, I stalked after him, realizing we needed to have a talk. But how and where? Getting him alone for such a chat would put me in a seriously compromised situation where I wouldn't be able to choose right. My flesh would rule, I had no doubt.

I should've been in a constant state of prayer while approaching the small table that held the marshmallows, chocolate pieces, and graham crackers. I should've been begging for His strength as I shoved my marshmallow-tipped stick close to the fire.

Heat singed my face as I stared at the flickering flames rather than acknowledging the too-young man a seat away from me doing the same.

I glanced at Chris's chair and found it empty.

Damnit.

I turned to scan the back yard, my gaze landing on and dismissing every kid in sight—including Marley who sat with a few other girls.

Jennifer hovered around the table, handing out s'mores supplies.

Shit.

I dropped my stick into the fire and stood.

Isaac whistled a song behind me as I stalked back toward the woods, but I didn't pay attention other than to noting he continued on with Kumbaya in perfect tune.

Quick, quiet footsteps took me back to where Isaac and I had collected our marshmallow sticks. I studied the direction I'd last seen Chris and Sara. A dozen or so strides deeper into the woods and I found them.

Lips locked, Chris's hand up Sara's shirt, her arms around his neck as he palmed her breast.

I cleared my throat, and they tore away from one another, Sara moving quicker than Chris who didn't seem to care as much about being caught. "Inside," I commanded, my tone hard. "Now."

My first true failing as a youth leader had my heart dropping into my stomach, guilt rising to fill my chest.

And since I couldn't have the other kids thinking I was a pushover, I decided on a harsh penalty for the two teens breaking the no-touch love teachings of the church.

Had it been a simple kiss, no seeking hands, I might have taken it a bit easier on them.

But I knew Chris, had been warned by Pastor Bram of the kid's reputation at the public school for chasing girls. Turned out, he'd gotten a young woman from the church pregnant a few years earlier.

At fifteen.

I sat them down in the living room and preached at them as the pastor would do—and made a few phone calls that ended their quasi-missions trip to Maine.

14

ISAAC

I whistled as loud as I could, the way I'd promised to do for Chris if he and Sara didn't make it back before Malachi noticed their absence. At least I'd managed to distract our youth leader, allowing the two to sneak off for a little bit of time.

My whistle to alert Chris didn't work.

Malachi stormed toward to the hostel a few minutes later, Chris and Sara on his heels, the little blonde's head hung in shame. Chris glanced my way, his lips in a tight line, and shook his head.

Fucking busted.

I wondered if he would rat me out for my part in helping him get her alone for the time they had. Lucky fuck had at least ten minutes with her. I hoped he'd at least gotten a handful of tits.

My first marshmallow burned, but I toasted two

more perfectly and scarfed them both down before Malachi returned.

Chris and Sara didn't.

He spoke a little while with Jennifer off to the side before she headed toward the hostel.

Malachi called the group around the fire to order and spoke a devotional like the leader always did for the nights we would be in Maine. His focus was on no-touch love. Obedience to God's word. Honoring those in authority.

Short, not sweet, and definitely unplanned— brought on by what had transpired in the woods, I didn't doubt.

I sat slouched in my chair like usual whenever someone preached, my arms crossed. Rather than staring into the fire and ignoring the words spoken, I gave Malachi my full attention. Stare unwavering. Silently begging him to look at me, to question his own stance on what he taught.

Think on how he'd kissed me.

Licked at my mouth.

Jerked off in the shower and stared at my stiff dick that afternoon like he'd wanted to touch. Taste. Take.

He didn't appear to remember jack shit and ignored my presence a seat away which annoyed the fuck out of me.

Jennifer never returned to the fire, so I didn't get asked to pull out my guitar from its case leaning against the back of my chair. I sure as fuck didn't offer.

When all the guys went upstairs later that night, Chris lay on his bunk, facing the wall.

I stripped down to my boxers, my attention on Malachi rather than my friend who didn't roll over to acknowledge any of us.

Keeping his back to me like he'd done prior to showering, Malachi pulled off his shirt, giving my drool factory something to get excited about. Rippling muscle beneath golden tan skin across his wide shoulders. Full-sleeved tattoos.

He pushed his jean shorts down, allowing me a nice view of his ass encased in blue boxer briefs that time—he flicked the lights off, leaving us in darkness, the memory of him etched in my mind.

I slid onto my bed, too hot to climb inside the sleeping bag.

Guys shifted around us getting comfortable, same as the night before, but most stayed quiet after the long day of laboring for our hosts. I stared at the empty bunk overhead, listening to Malachi breathe beside me, mere feet away.

Snores and heaving exhales eventually filled the room, and still I lay wide awake, my skin buzzing with awareness.

Turning my head, I could barely make out the image of Malachi from the room's lone window beyond him, an old curtain allowing in a sliver of moonlight.

Eyes open, he too stared overhead. Pecs prominent, hands clasped on his stomach. The bulge beneath his torso caused my fingertips to itch. I shifted on my cot-like mattress, my dick's growing discomfort making it difficult to get comfortable.

Malachi turned his head toward me, but his face lay in shadow. "Go to sleep, Isaac," he whispered, my groin tightening at hearing him say my name.

"Can't," I whispered back.

He didn't move, didn't speak, and I wondered how clearly he could see my face, my eyes in the darkness. Did he look at the outline of my body? I slid my hand down over my stomach to rearrange my own bulge, even though it wasn't restricted by tight briefs. Good thing, boxers.

Malachi's breath caught, and I smirked, giving myself an extra squeeze, enough that my hips lifted.

"Isaac," he warned, his own lower half moving on his mattress.

"Hmm?"

"Go to sleep."

I released my dick and let out a heavy exhale, facing away from him so he could check out my ass all he wanted.

No whispered curse rose like I'd hoped to hear, but I caught the rustle of material, like he adjusted the ache I'd caused.

At least, that was what I hoped for. Pretty sure I still smirked when I drifted off fuck knew how much later.

———

The next morning while we ate breakfast, Chris's and Sara's dads showed up together at the hostel's front door.

My jaw stopped working to chew the Raisin Bran we'd been offered for breakfast in those single-serve boxes I needed four of to fill my stomach.

Chris hadn't looked at me that morning and hadn't spoken a word to me, even when I'd whispered his name while we'd been getting dressed for the day. He'd merely shaken his head and disappeared into the bathroom.

He didn't come down for breakfast, and I realized when his dad walked in that Malachi had taken consequences to the extreme.

He'd sent the two to bed early the night before, not allowing them further interaction with the group. He'd called their dads to come pick them up. Didn't allow either Chris or Sara to come to breakfast, I noted, glancing around the girls' table to find her absent too.

Malachi motioned the two men into the living room and around the corner.

The rest of us in the kitchen/dining area

remained quiet while eating, everyone glancing around and wondering what was going on even though it was obvious. The sound of plastic spoons on plastic bowls and chewing were the only silence breakers.

Jennifer sat at the end of the table, seemingly caught up in her own cereal.

Murmured voices reached us, but even with me being the closest to the three men, I couldn't make out what they said.

Minutes later, Chris and Sara followed their dads out the hostel's front door, their bags in hand. Feet shuffling, their heads downcast.

No one questioned why they would leave without looking our way or saying goodbye. No one's voice rose in inquiry about what had happened that was so terrible Malachi would send them home.

But rumors abounded throughout the day as we got to work. Malachi's thin-lipped scowl and silence reminded me so much of my own dad when disappointed that my stomach cramped.

Could have been the Raisin Bran, but my guts churned at how he'd handled the situation. It wasn't like he'd caught them fucking. I doubted Chris would have talked Sara into letting him have her virginity out in the woods, a mere ten minutes into their first time alone.

For a simple kiss? Maybe not so simple?

Had she gone down on him or had he buried his face between her thighs?

Who the hell knew—all sorts of whispered ideas rose from the other teens whenever Malachi and Miss Jennifer weren't in close proximity.

Eventually, my anger, my disgust over how he'd done exactly as my dad would have rose to the point that I couldn't look at him. I avoided him when we finished the rock wall and went down to the lake to cool off with a swim, one of the things I usually enjoyed the most seeing as how I'd spent lots of time at my family's cottage on Lake Wallenpaupack.

I sat with my journal in hand, scribbling nonsensical pissiness while the other kids splashed and laughed, Chris and Sara seemingly forgotten.

Even the sight of sun-kissed skin and tattoos down our youth pastor's right arm couldn't hold me enthralled.

Malachi Foley was a judgmental asshole, a fucking liar of the worst sort.

And I was so over him.

15

———————

MALACHI

Isaac ignored me the next couple of days, making the hours longer and the evenings even more brutal. I'd planned nightly devotionals, but the interest he'd shown with his hazel-eyed stare the first night I spoke around the campfire had vanished, and it bothered the shit out of me.

And then...then he played his guitar at Jennifer's insistence while the ring of kids around him sang. Lips pursed, he plucked notes, strummed like a goddamn pro, drawing me deeper into his grasp. Giving me breath. Desire beyond the physical.

My heart ached to join him, to hear his talent, knowing his dreams would take him far away— which was best, for me at least.

Him, I doubted, but more out of fear due to his flirting nature that had completely cut off toward me during those days of laboring in the sun for the glory of God.

I hated how he wouldn't acknowledge me when I should have rejoiced that he'd appeared to have gotten over his pursuit of what could never be.

I loved that he slept beside me. Cursed that I couldn't reach out and touch, to span the short distance separating our bunks.

My gut hardened over the decision to send Chris and Sara home, and I didn't doubt Isaac's anger stemmed from taking his one friend from him, but it'd been necessary—as a warning to myself, not just the teens.

Isaac had too much talent and was too beautiful to end up six feet under in an early grave like Brian. Spewing the shit of my past and the reasons I denied us would have opened his eyes, but I also would have ousted my biggest sin, the part of me that would keep me from serving God in the future like I'd promised my mom.

Isaac sulked in his passive aggressive way, but I wouldn't relent in my silence or refusal to give him attention outside of sharing God's Word with him in a group setting.

Like a petulant child with his candy taken away, he pouted, dragging his feet about helping around the hostel or taking his part in whatever chores he'd been assigned.

And that lower lip tempted me to the point of

pain. I woke every morning with a raging hard on. Jacked off in the shower soon after crawling out of bed and a second time once the day's work finished.

Yet still I ached, my heart and mind just as much as my body.

With guilt, with concern for his withdrawal from the rest of the group. While the rest of us swam in the lake, he sat off alone. While we all sprawled around the campfire and shared ghost stories and memories of past retreats, he picked at his fingernails or imaginary lint off his jeans. At least he continued to play his guitar for our time of worship, and every night, I tried not to stare while soaking his talent—his gift—in.

With proper guidance, he could make it big in Nashville. Half Korean, his beauty would catch attention. Add in his broody nature, that "it" factor agents and record labels looked for, and I didn't doubt his successful future.

And I hadn't even heard him sing. But I could imagine how he'd sound, considering the natural husk to his voice and how well he'd whistled that first night I'd sent Chris and Sara home.

But how to point Isaac in the correct direction? How could I encourage him on the right path if he wouldn't even acknowledge me or the words of my nightly teachings?

Our final night in Maine we went out beneath starlit skies, crickets and night insects' calls rising enough to be heard over the fire I helped our host create. I ended up beside Isaac somehow—not my doing—for the devotional.

The scent of cinnamon clung to him and filled my nose.

Clearing my throat, I glanced around our circle of kids, smiling. Jennifer beamed at me from a few seats away on my right.

"Tonight we're going to talk about showing others grace and mercy."

"Like you did Chris?" Isaac muttered under his breath, his first words to me in days.

I ignored him, hoping others hadn't heard while opening my Bible on my lap to the passage I'd book-marked earlier in the book of Micah. Guilt and anger mingled together in my head, and I fought them off before beginning the evening's message.

I read a highlighted verse in chapter seven which spoke of God pardoning sin and forgiving transgressions. How His anger didn't last, but His mercy did.

Isaac let out a quiet snort, and I paused, considering calling him out for his disrespectful behavior.

But I chose mercy, understanding he was pissed off over his only friend being sent home.

I kept my Bible open but lifted my gaze to the faces turned my way, the apt focus I knew I would only have for a few moments before attention spans ended and the shifting began.

Feelings of incompetence rose as I preached the

Word to a bunch of impressionable kids. Ones, I hoped still had yet to make life-changing choices like I'd done.

My stomach twisted as flashes of my memory, my past sins, filled my head, and I ended the devotional sooner than planned, looking to Jennifer to start our time of singing.

"Isaac?" she asked, leaning forward to catch sight of him on my other side. "Would you play for us again tonight?"

He didn't answer, and I forced my focus on his face.

More imaginary lint disappeared off his jeans, and I glanced at the back of his chair. No guitar propped against it as it had been in the previous couple of nights. "Isaac."

"What?" He snipped, glaring at me when he lifted his head.

Our gazes clashed, heat and energy rippling between us that I feared others would notice.

"Jennifer asked if you would play for our singing tonight," I stated, keeping my tone conversational when I wanted to throttle the brat. Kiss his mouth. Bite his nipples. Fondle his—

"Nope." He popped the P.

"Go get your guitar," I ordered quietly, fighting the desire to grab hold of his shirt and shake the shit out of him. "Now."

His eyes narrowed, but he hopped up, his folding chair toppling, and he stormed toward the hostel.

Jennifer stood to go after him, but I grasped her arm. "I'll talk to him."

I righted his overturned chair, my stomach hard, knowing as the authority figure I had to do something, say something.

Even if heading into a dark building—alone— could lead to my fall from grace.

Or maybe he didn't want me anymore with how he'd changed after I'd sent Chris and Sara home. I hoped yet hated that might be the case.

The hostel sat quiet, making my exhales loud. I stood in the entryway, the dim kitchen on my right, the living area on the opposite, and the stairs leading upward beyond the lamp's glow left on at an end table beside a couch.

Darkness shaded the top of the hallway, the way to the second floor impenetrable by a human's eye.

The path represented so much more than mere stairs in my mind, but I didn't have a choice. Prayers should have whispered in my head, ones of delivery and protection against temptation, but my thoughts sat quiet, no whispered pleas for help from an omniscient God.

Perhaps Isaac would descend—I could wait for him there, and we could talk in the light of the living room. No noise sounded from overhead, so I filled my lungs and crossed the room with sure steps, even though my heart faltered and my legs shook.

My lips pressed into a thin line as I moved up the stairs, the muffled singing voices outside letting me know the youth group continued on without us.

"Isaac?" I called out as I neared the top of the stairs.

He didn't answer, and I turned into the open room housing the guys' bunks to find him sitting on the floor between our beds, knees drawn up and head against the wall.

Even in the dim light filtering through the window, I could see he scowled at me. "What?"

"I told you to get your guitar."

"I'm not playing tonight."

I stayed put in the entryway, fighting my body's desire to go to him. But we needed to talk and not with a bed hindering my view of his face.

I rounded my bunk and hesitated at the end, less than eight feet separating us as I stood over him, hands shoving into my jeans' pockets.

"What's the problem?" I asked, expecting he needed to unload his anger on me in order for us to move forward.

"I want you." His pissy tone suggested he hated that fact.

A lack of desire filled his one eye unhidden by shadow, but his words punched like a fist to my gut, stealing my breath all the same.

"You're too young to know that," I spewed with a ragged voice rather than admitting the truth.

"I'm *legal*," he shot back, "and I know *you* want *me*."

I lifted my chin, attempting to give him the same haughty look. "I don't."

"Liar." He stood, putting us on more an even level, and I stilled all except for my dick swelling with life of its own. Every cell in my body tensed, and even though I slid my hands out of my pockets, I readied to fight rather than flee which would've have been smarter.

Three steps brought him within touching distance, and we both breathed heavily, staring through the charged air simmering between us. Hands fisted, I trembled as his focus slipped down to my mouth.

My lips tingled at the memory of his touching mine. Tongues dueling. His panted breaths against my mouth, the sweetness of cinnamon I wanted to inhale until he filled my lungs fully.

"Liar," he whispered again, moving one last step.

Mere inches separated us.

Long eyelashes blinked, the lust for sin in his eyes tightening my balls against my body.

My mind emptied of all rational thought, 3 dictating my brainwaves.

His hands touched my hips as I lowered my head

to suck his exhale into my lungs. Lips hovered close, hot breath mingling.

Need. So fucking *much—*

I moved with force, taking his mouth in a bruising kiss, one hand reaching up his back to grasp his neck, the other on his ass as I shoved him, slamming his back and my forearms against the wall.

Lithe muscle pressed against me rather than melting, our fight for more one of unrestrained passion rather than submission, and that lit my skin on fire. Shoving my tongue into his mouth earned me a whimpered moan that had pre-cum leaking from my dick, but he didn't relax in my arms, didn't just let me have my way with him like Brian had always done.

His hunger for me rivaled mine for him, the kind that consumed. Burned.

Isaac fumbled at my zipper with desperate fingers, muffled curses against my mouth until he got the access he wanted. No hesitation—the kid shoved his hand beneath my boxer's waistband, going straight for my dick.

His firm grip closed around me, causing my length to jerk in his hold and my entire body to shudder.

I cursed against his mouth, his hand sheer torture, fingers soft...so fucking perfect.

More.

I released his ass to grab his dick through his shorts.

"Oh fuck." He gasped, ripping his mouth from mine to lean his head against the wall.

I stared at his hooded eyes while we both panted, my hand squeezing him hidden by darkness.

"Fuck...touch it. Touch me. Please."

My fingers didn't shake while yanking open his zipper and shoving his shorts and boxers to mid-thigh.

"Oh shit." He gulped, losing his hold on my length as I put space enough between us to push mine down as well.

My entire body a raging furnace, I came at him like a rabid dog, taking his lips again. Pressing our groins together, swallowing his whimpers as I closed my fist around our dicks.

Enough pre-cum from both of us coated my hand, the kind of slickness that created one hell of a fist fuck. He shuddered as I jerked us off, my tongue fucking his mouth in time with my hand gliding over hot, hard flesh.

My heartbeat pounded in my ears as lust over-rode all my senses.

Nothing but trouble would come from our sins, but in that heated moment of passion flaring between us, I didn't care. Couldn't. Too much need had built up, and I had no strength to deny him.

Us.

We'd been on the edge of combustion since meeting. Karma, fate, temptation...whatever had brought our lonely souls together couldn't be set aside for someone else's greater good. Selfishness led —and I followed.

16

ISAAC

Over Malachi Foley, my ass.

A sense of breathlessness lightened my head, and I turned my face away from the demanding mouth I'd told myself the past couple of days I didn't want in order to fill my lungs.

My hips thrust in time with his downward tug over our lengths pressed tightly together. I'd dreamed of his hands on me, our dicks in his grasp, his hot breath on my neck. The reality of Malachi and me together shattered all my porn-fed fantasies.

Silk and steel, slick...ball tingling perfection that flooded my mouth with drool.

"Fuck. Oh fuck." I swallowed hard, the feel of his hard length against mine, heat, wetness...his firm grip foreign and knee-weakening.

"Mmm," he moaned his agreement, the rumble of his chest drawing my balls up tight.

"G-gonna come, Malachi. Fucking hell," I gasped, thrusting and trembling.

"Yes," he groaned, peering down between us. "I want to see it."

Too dark—too damn dark.

I stared like he did, trying to make out what I could hear, the schlicking noise of a pre-cum soaked hand sliding and twisting, rubbing and tugging. Panting, I fought off the brewing in my balls, the impending explosion.

Doomed.

No power.

"Give it to me, Isaac," he whispered against my ear, all rasp and sex.

At the first sense of cum erupting, I grabbed hold of Malachi's head and brought his mouth back to mine. My teeth clanked against his, our tongues wrestling as we rutted against each other. He swallowed my grunted whimpers, pressing me tight to the wall.

My dick jerked in his fist, spurting.

Head spinning, I mentally spewed curses, trembling in Malachi's hold. My entire body shook, threatening to drop me to my knees.

"Yes," he groaned again and shuddered, wetness smearing between our groins as he milked us both with a firm grip, coaxing every last dribble from our lengths. "Christ..."

Gasping, he tilted his forehead against mine, sharing the air between our lips as my fingers stayed speared in his silky hair.

Every muscle in my body went lax, his hard mass keeping me in place.

"Fuck," he whispered harshly, giving our flagging lengths one last pull.

"Mmm," I agreed, soaking in the tingles racing over my skin, through my blood. Mind empty, I breathed in the scent of his soap and dryer sheets, my hands sliding down to hold his shoulders.

Muscles bunched beneath his T-shirt under my touch.

A shudder rippled through me as a sigh escaped, my lips curving upward over Malachi giving me another first.

So. Fucking. Good.

He stepped away, leaving me sagging against the wall, and my wet groin cooled without his touch.

"Damnit." He ran his clean hand through his hair, down over his face, the rasp of his palm against whiskers making me want to feel them on the backs of my thighs while he ate my ass.

My smile widened. "Deny you want me now."

Like a heavy fog falling down over my head, I could see the shroud of guilt blanket him, and my triumphant grin faded, a frigid chill replacing the warmth inside me.

Malachi looked away, his head lowered.

"Don't." I bit out the word—but he stalked off toward the bathroom before I could beg him to not erect a wall of regret between us.

Water ran, and I couldn't move, my entire body as spent as my limp dick still hanging out in the open. I watched the bathroom door. Waited for him to decide his thoughts and feelings on what we'd done.

Malachi returned with a handful of wet paper towels but kept his distance, his expression closed off. Hard, from what I could see from the moonlight filtering through the window.

My heart seized inside my chest.

He'd cleaned up. Zippered up. "You need to change." His husky voice twitched my dick as I glanced down.

We'd made a mess of my favorite green shirt.

I ripped it off overhead, my hand shaking as I balled it up and tossed it into my dirty laundry bag beside me.

He gave me the wet towels, and I muttered a thanks while taking them from him to clean myself. Heart like a lump of stone in my chest, I wiped up, and he rifled through my gym bag at the foot of my bed for a clean shirt.

"We shouldn't have done that," he whispered, remorse lining his voice and twisting my guts up tight, erasing the after-tingles I usually enjoyed from emptying my balls.

I tucked my dick away, wanted to argue, but what could I say that would sway him to my side?

A youth pastor jerking off the pastor's son in a hot as fuck make out session.

Even I could see the taboo in that.

It didn't make me want him any less though.

"This can't happen again, Isaac." Hardness edged his tone, and I finally lifted my gaze to his.

He tossed me a clean shirt.

His eyes promised we wouldn't, that he refused to even think on it.

Malachi voiced his desired fate for us, but I'd broken him down once. I could do it again.

While I pulled on my shirt, he bent to retrieve my guitar from beneath my bunk.

"I need a few moments alone," he muttered, handing me my case.

I wanted to assure him that we *would* happen again, that I wouldn't rest until I made it so.

Malachi could stand firm and beg his God for forgiveness each and every time we came together, but we would.

I refused to think anything contrary.

Without another word, I brushed passed him, my knees weak but my steps light rather than dragging with guilt like his probably did. I rode the high of having the best orgasm of my life, and nothing would take it from me.

I could still taste Malachi on my lips and smell a hint of dryer sheets. Curling my fingers into a fist, I attempted to hang onto the feel of his hair against my palm.

Our dicks, hot and wet, gliding together in the best fist fuck a man could have.

Warmth flushed through me from head to toes at the memory of his groans, his hot breath ghosting over my neck.

Shit, I need to calm the fuck down.

Biting back my grin, I rounded the hostel into view of the campfire and the others still singing.

Miss Jennifer's smile lit as she caught sight of me, her lips faltering to stay tilted up as she glanced behind me and found Malachi absent. Fuck, how I wanted to brag about leaving him sated up in the guys' bunks.

Instead, I sat on my chair and pulled out my guitar. Plucked a few notes, adjusting what needed to be set straight while breathing in the woodsmoke and night air, and I found the key the youth group sang in, my playing taking over the lead.

But I didn't hear a goddamn word coming from their mouths. I got lost in the strings of my guitar while reliving what Malachi and I had just shared. Hopefully, the first of many such run-ins.

We finished a minute later, and Miss Jennifer thanked me.

They sang another song while I accompanied them, but still Malachi didn't join us.

Had he dropped to his knees to pray? Cried tears of repentance for putting his hands on me? Eating at my mouth and swallowing my cries while he brought us both to orgasm?

The first not of my hand...

My lips twitched for the tenth or so time since leaving him upstairs, and I wondered if he knew that truth while Miss Jennifer's soprano praised God.

Deciding I needed to tell him that I wanted him to have *all* my firsts, I kept playing when the praise song ended and morphed it into one I'd written. A cryptic song that if the meaning wasn't known could be taken as God and church approved.

Well, it'd been written as a worship song—just not to the One my company thought worthy of.

The other kids stayed quiet in the night, Miss Jennifer allowing me to pluck a tune I'd written in the previous month that had nothing to do with God but his creation. The man of my obsession.

But they wouldn't know. The obscure words could be taken either way.

Still riding the high of release, I closed my eyes, the decision coming as easily as Malachi had pulled my orgasm from my body.

The crackle of the fire accompanied my song—

my voice—rising into the night, and with my eyes closed, I sang praises to him, my muse.

The one who drew me in.

Broken and bleeding.

Needing what only he could give.

But he wasn't capitalized like a proper noun, simply a man. The one I longed to worship.

The one my soul craved.

17

———

MALACHI

Devastation had me sinking into my bunk, and I sat hunched over, my elbows on knees and my head in my hands.

Failure. Sin.

Of the worst possible sort.

Kissing Isaac in the janitor's closet had been bad enough, but touching his flesh? Lusting for it? Hearing and feeling him come undone in my arms, his hard, lithe body pressed against my front?

Hell.

Eyes dry, I lifted my head to heaven, peering into darkness and wondering if the Holy Spirit intervened for me like the Word promised for those who didn't have the strength to pray.

So weak to the lusts of the flesh.

"Put on the whole armor of God," I repeated what I'd preached dozens of times, the encouragement I gave the teens to help them face life's decisions. Easier said than done.

If we didn't plan to leave the next morning, I would have called Pastor Bram and told him to come get his son like I'd done with Chris and Sara's fathers. Knowing I didn't have the strength to deny us, I needed him far from my sight, my reach.

And yet my heart hurt for him. I understood his circumstances, the attraction to men, the desperate desire for attention—both of which I suffered from as well.

I craved physical touch like I required breath. Wanted words of affirmation and edification spoken out loud rather than read between the pages of a leatherbound, God-inspired, Bible.

No spirit of God filled me. No sense of peace in mentally acknowledging my sins I couldn't speak out loud and couldn't beg forgiveness for.

Longing for Isaac's nearness and feeling more alone than I ever had, I got to my feet. Hurried down the stairs and into the night.

Just damn *needing*.

I caught the sound of a guitar first.

Then a male voice, one I recognized even though I'd never heard Isaac sing.

Rounding the hostel, I pulled up short as his husky tenor swept over me.

Not a song I knew, but I stood unmoving, breath and stare ensnared, caught up in the purity of his tone. The rasp that would make anyone swoon, male or female alike.

Jennifer and the kids sat still as stone, staring at Isaac as he lifted his voice into the spark-lit night, the stars overhead baptizing his dark head.

Desire swelled in the deepest parts of my soul, beyond physical lust, beyond wanting affection. His tone swirled inside my head, descended through my body, and caught me up in a vortex I couldn't stop even if God lassoed His righteousness around my chest to hold me back.

Isaac's eyes opened, and his focus turned toward me as though he felt my stare, that mouth, those lips still moving and pouring magic from his lungs. Tempting me to believe the truth of the song he'd written.

He sang his words of brokenness and longing to *me*—not God like the others doubtless believed.

Broken.

Bleeding.

His tone rasped, ripping through my chest as our gazes held.

Wanting to fall. Worship you.

Needing you.

Without words to beg for your touch.

I stood struck dumb. Enthralled. My body responded to the lure of his voice, manipulating my desires as easily as his fingers strummed the guitar's strings.

His voice and the notes faded into the dark night too damn soon, leaving a buzz in my ears as our gazes remained locked in the sudden stillness. My entire body tingled to erase the distance between us. I craved his exhales to flood my lungs, craved to slide my lips over his skin. To lick and taste. Fill up my mind, my soul, with everything he would allow me.

Hoots, hollers, and clapping erupted, blinking me back to reality, tearing my focus off his face.

The fire burned bright yellow and gold in the night as though reaching for heaven, sparks fading up into darkness overhead.

Disappearing, their lives snuffed out.

As though they never existed, the memory of them fading with every heartbeat thumping in my ears.

"Malachi," Jennifer called, and I forced a smile and my feet forward, every inch of my body *alive*.

I took the seat I'd emptied earlier, putting me beside Isaac who still sat with his guitar in hand.

Electric waves pulsed from him, raising the hairs on my arms even though I refused to look at him. Rubbing my palms over my jean shorts, I told myself to get a hold on my thoughts, the tumbling desires lighting me up like a damn rainbow after the rain clouds dissipated.

"Will you sing another?" Jennifer asked Isaac, and the kids all piped up their request.

Isaac didn't say a word surprisingly but started

playing without his usual rebellious attitude, his head bent over his guitar.

A tune I recognized emerged rather than a hidden-meaning song he'd written for me, thank God.

I let out a heavy exhale and closed my eyes, trying to focus on the words he sang about being beautifully created. Wholly accepted. Not a more popular worship hymn, not specifically mentioning God. A song that could be taken as a love ballad had it not been created by one of contemporary Christian music's most popular singers.

Some kids joined in the chorus, but most simply listened to the perfection of Isaac's voice.

Chords from the song rose inside me, and I hummed along without thought. Another verse...the chorus...my lips parted, and I joined with him, our voices entwining as we sang in the kind of pure harmony I'd only heard once before.

Pain lanced through my chest, but I couldn't stop, couldn't contain the draw to sing along with Isaac and create such utter perfection my entire body ached.

The others fell silent around us, but I kept my eyes closed, blending my voice with his. Basked in the warmth radiating inside me—and not the peace of God in the purity of worship. Adrenaline rushed through my veins, seeming to wake my soul and cause my heartbeat to drum in my chest.

Our notes wove together, tight. In unity—as though our souls entwined, never to be put asunder.

A sudden release of tension, of guilt, of remorse left me lightheaded.

Giddy.

Wanting to grin like a fool in love...

I breathed smoke-scented air easily between the lines we sang together, the oxygen a life-giving force that tingled my extremities. My lips smiled on their own, a lack of tension and stress loosening my muscles.

No desire to escape filled me. I *lived* in the moment, wanting to spread my arms wide to hold onto the sense of happiness flooding through me.

Pure joy, the kind I'd been searching for my whole life. The kind God's word promised but hadn't ever gifted.

Our song ended.

And wild applause ensued.

I opened my eyes and met Isaac's stare. His soft expression, the flush on his cheeks, and his relaxed posture brought on a craving for *more* that had me shifting in my seat.

"That was amazing!" Jennifer gushed, her grasp on my arm pulling me away from the person I wanted to lose myself in.

Reality slapped me like a hand to the face, and I blinked her into focus as my heart stuttered.

"The two of you...just wow! Seriously, the two of you sound beautiful together!"

We would be *beautiful together.*

"You need to sing a duet in church. Holy cow..." Jennifer's voice faded from my consciousness as I glanced around the ring of kids, the firelight playing on their smiling faces.

Filled with the love of God, wrapped up in emotionalism.

Isaac and I had done that for them through song —but neither of our hearts had been in the right place when singing the words meant to praise our maker.

The thought hit me like an axe to the chest, stealing my joy entirely. Sweat broke out on my brow, and thickness in my throat kept me from swallowing hard like I needed to do.

Immorality. An abomination.

My pulse raced over the truth that the wages of sin was death, and I jerked my head back toward Isaac to find him tucking his guitar away. I'd been responsible for one young man's demise.

No way in hell would I send another there to burn for all eternity.

———

I became the avoider, staying as far away from Isaac as possible. And my heart ached because of it, the hollowness in my chest intensifying to the point I often gasped from the pain.

The draw of him, the longing in my soul to sing, to touch, to taste, was more than I could fight in close proximity.

Once home from our retreat, moving through daily living proved easier. With school out, the only time I had to feel the energy between us that my soul craved was Sunday morning worship and Wednesday night youth group.

The first Sunday, I stayed away from him until I couldn't. He exited the church's front doors rather than sneaking out the side like usual with Chris and Tyler.

Every member of the church walked through the line, bringing him closer. My pulse thrummed, making me hyperaware of the buzz of energy swirling inside me.

"Malachi," he stated in greeting, raising the hairs on my arms beneath my suit. His eyes studied my face as I offered him a brief nod, shaking his hand and pulling it back as quickly as possible.

My entire body itched to haul him toward me, wrap him up in my arms, and take all his worries, his future hurts onto my own shoulders.

I moved my attention to the couple beyond him rather than responding to his greeting, smiling and thanking them for coming that morning.

Isaac moved off, leaving a crushing weight on

my chest. I couldn't breathe and didn't have the focus or energy to disregard the shame of being an asshole.

Guilt crept in.

As his youth pastor, it was my duty to encourage, edify, and love the teenagers—including Isaac. Shunning him was unacceptable.

But I couldn't find it in me to seek him out to apologize. Doing so would only put us in a compromising situation I feared I'd fail.

Wednesday, he sat silent in his folded chair while the kids sang, their voices echoing in the gymnasium. No guitar. Arms crossed, slouched like a brat once he realized I refused to interact with him. I ignored his whispers with Chris and Tyler, his attempts to gain my attention. I ignored the urge to talk to him since I couldn't discern the Holy Spirit's guidance from my fleshly desires.

The next week passed in the same manner, my feigned disinterest obvious enough that Isaac didn't even look at me, thank God.

That Friday, I breathed a bit easier, knowing I still had forty-eight hours before having to bear his presence, his stares from the congregation again.

Pastor Bram knocked on my office door, poking his head in when I called out for him to enter. "Busy?" he asked with a smile.

I shook my head, grateful for the interruption of thoughts I couldn't keep from wandering toward his son—and the pastor's ignorance over what had transpired between us. "Come on in."

His smile faltered as he sat in the chair across my desk. "So, Isaac…"

I stilled, fighting to keep my smile in place, my eyes unshielded or burdened by guilt. I also knew better than to open my mouth, so I let him work through whatever he wanted to say to me as a few tense minutes passed.

"He's really struggling. More than usual." Pastor Bram lifted his eyes to the ceiling as though in silent prayer for his son. "I know all I can do is trust God to lead his steps, but I'm finding it difficult to even think about Isaac going off to a whole other state without guidance. No matter how much truth or scripture I give him, he's unresponsive. He'll be eighteen in a few weeks, and I can't force him to stay here at home. I'm deeply troubled for his soul."

As was I—for both of us—but I kept my thoughts to myself.

"I was wondering if you would meet with him in a non-church setting," Pastor Bram continued, glancing my way once more. "Become his friend rather than just his youth pastor if possible. Maybe he'd be willing to open up to you if you build a rapport outside these doors."

A close relationship.

If only he knew how close we'd already become, the feelings and the push and pull between us that had filled the night with gorgeous harmony when we'd been in Maine.

I cleared my throat while smoothing down my tie, knowing I didn't have a choice. My boss, my pastor, wanted me to counsel his son which meant God led me toward that path. I had to trust His light would steer my way, even though I feared it would end in my destruction.

"I can do that, yes, but I'd prefer to meet him here in my office if that's okay with you." Doing so would keep us from sinning again—I hoped. At least being on holy ground would make it easier for me to turn away from temptation.

Pastor Bram's face lit with the joy of the Lord. "Thank you."

He wouldn't be thanking me if he knew what trouble his son and I managed to get into when alone.

18

ISAAC

To top off the bullshit of my life, Dad and I got into it over Nashville.

Again.

And Mom sat silent at the dinner table Saturday night, refusing to back me up or even encourage Dad to just listen to what I had to say.

Aggravation kept me on edge, got my mind going. Only a couple weeks lay between me and my eighteenth birthday, but what held me back from leaving right away? With Dad and his focus on all things law and doing right, I expected he'd contact the police about me being a runaway or some shit.

But by the time they would catch up to me, I'd probably have turned eighteen.

Who else would attempt to stop me from seeking freedom early?

"It's too risky heading into the unknown," Dad

repeated what he'd said before, but I didn't tell him I already had a plan, that I knew where I would go and what I would do. "If you need a year off from studies, stay here. Immerse yourself in God's word. Seek his will for your life before starting Bible college next fall."

I shoveled more mashed potatoes into my mouth to keep from telling him exactly what I thought about *his* plans for my life and how opposite they were from mine.

I ought to pack my bags and take off the second they fall asleep.

The idea made my blood race, but I couldn't leave without seeing Malachi again. I needed that opportunity to have him, to finish what we'd started. My body, my mind—my damn heart—demanded it, no matter how much I told myself I didn't want him, didn't like what he'd chosen to be.

I'd ridden a high from being with him in Maine, hearing his voice weave with mine—fucking magic.

But his avoidance of me began immediately after that bonfire. He wouldn't look at me as I'd laid in my bunk, staring at him until drifting off. He wouldn't talk to me after his regrets of getting us both off. The heaviness in my chest dragged my feet.

"I've set up a meeting for you and Malachi." Dad's firm tone would usually make me scowl.

I stopped chewing my steak, eyeing my dad. My stomach twisted up tight as fuck over whatever it was he had planned—or what the youth pastor might have told him.

"Since you won't share personal stuff with either of us," Dad said, motioning between him and Mom, "I thought he would be the next best choice."

Shit.

I released my held breath and finished chewing my mouthful of food. The cramp in my gut over the fear of being found out dissipated as quickly as it'd started, even though the adrenaline left me a little shaky.

Having Malachi all to myself behind closed doors? Yes, please and thank you. I didn't care where we got the chance to be alone, just that we would before I left.

"When?" I asked, trying to not show too much enthusiasm.

"Tomorrow morning before service," Dad said, his lips immediately thinning.

The disappointment lining his face no longer bothered me. Knowing what I did about myself, what I refused to share with my parents, ensured it was all I would ever be to the Bible-thumping, dogmatic ass who'd donated sperm to help give me life.

I nodded, acknowledging the meeting, and went back to eating, trying to hide the tremors in my hands.

A chance to have Malachi bend me over his desk.

Fuck into my ass slow and deep, taking what I craved to gift him more than anything. I wanted him more than I did Nashville.

And the clash of that truth in my mind kept me awake long into the night, leaving me adrift, like I bobbed in an ocean with no land in sight. The clench of my guts returned as I worried over a man who'd turned my world upside down. Took first place over my dreams.

But I didn't regret it.

Malachi Foley made me feel...*things* I didn't understand. Couldn't name or even put into words. I just knew that no matter how much having him in my life had fucked shit up, I wouldn't have gone back to change the past even if I could.

At two in the morning, I grabbed my journal and spewed a bunch of gibberish even I couldn't make sense of.

Once I finished, my soul emptied, and I closed my eyes and dreamed about a reality where I got everything I wanted. A record deal. Screaming fans who accepted me exactly as I was.

And Malachi.

Beside me in my bed, loving me without hesitation. Unconditionally.

———

I drove to church with Dad the next morning, staring out the passenger window rather than having bagels and cream cheese with Mom. Trees whipped past as he quietly talked to me about sharing and being open with my thoughts and emotions. He encouraged me to be honest with a man who could be more than a youth pastor to me.

But after the dreams I'd floated in while sleeping, I would never be satisfied having Malachi for a mere friend. I *wanted* him to be more.

So much more.

Clamping my lips as though I agreed with Dad kept him from raising his voice at me. But I barely listened anyway since my heart raced and my thoughts filled with the "what ifs" over the meeting ahead. Damp palms, itching skin...I felt like I had hives, and nothing I did calmed my insides.

We pulled into the church's lot, pebbles crunching beneath the tires.

Malachi's old truck parked in his assigned spot, a pile of rust and mismatched quarter panels of various colors. Not the kind of vehicle I expected Dad approved of for a man in authority at a church, but I sure as hell did.

The truck sat imperfect.

Showing signs of having lived powerlessly beneath an onslaught of weather dished out on it.

Kinda sexy even.

My lips quirked as I climbed from Dad's car.

"Please be open with him," Dad stated for at least the tenth time, solidifying my desire to say absolutely jack shit to Malachi about anything personal. I wanted his dick, nothing more, since reality would never live up to my dreams, same as I would never be good enough for Dad.

I grunted a response he could take however he wanted while following him into the church's foyer.

The scent of lemon cleaner burned my nose, but I kept my lips sealed so I wouldn't taste the chemicals meant to scrub and cleanse germs from every surfaced touched by the flesh of man.

The smell offended my senses—same as Dad's bullshit spewed from the pulpit.

Breathing deep and slowly exhaling didn't ease the tension riding my shoulders and making my legs shake.

I'd jerked off twice while in the shower so Dad wouldn't see me sporting a boner, but even an hour later, my dick chubbed up at the thought of having Malachi behind closed doors. Alone. Just him and me and the connection linking our souls.

Dad knocked on his office door, and when Malachi told us to enter, he pushed it in and stepped back.

"Be open," Dad murmured as I stepped past him.

I nodded, my focus going to Malachi behind his desk. He wore a light blue dress shirt, striped tie...

freshly shaven cheeks, lips in a thin line as he shuffled paperwork on his desk.

Dad closed the door behind me, and I shifted on my feet, waiting for Malachi to acknowledge me. To give me his eyes. The attention I yearned for.

The hives feeling returned, and I recognized the craving to have him putting his hands on me and showing me the kind of affection my body and mind lusted over.

"Have a seat," Malachi said, focusing on the shit atop his desk.

I forced steady breaths while sitting in the chair across from him, every cell in my body buzzing from the close proximity. Chin tilted upward, I waited. Gaze locked on him.

He closed his eyes a moment and stilled—probably praying for strength, for wisdom.

My lips twitched, hoping God didn't hear his pleadings.

A heavy exhale and Malachi lifted his head.

We stared at one another in the silence, my arm hairs raising regardless of his shuttered eyes. Trouble lined his face, like his will battled the lusts of the flesh. His fingers clasped atop some papers, knuckles white as though he fought to keep from reaching for me.

Giving us what we both wanted.

"Did your father tell you why you're here?" he asked, his tone level, almost...reluctant.

The only time he'd acted differently toward me was when he had his hands on my body.

My dick twitched as I considered ways to get those fingers ghosting over my skin and his lower lip between my teeth.

"He wants us to be friends," I stated what couldn't happen platonically.

"And you know that can never be."

Well at least the struggling man decided to shoot straight for a change, saying exactly what I'd expected.

"I disagree," I said. "I think we can be friends and a hell of a lot more if you'd pull your head out of your ass."

"Isaac."

"Ask me what I want." I sat forward, elbows on my knees, holding his gaze. "Ask me how we can move forward...because I have all sorts of ideas."

Fuck, did I ever.

Malachi cleared his throat, glancing away and back again as though hitting return on his laptop. "When do you head to Nashville?"

Sure enough, he'd started a new paragraph, poking at my insecurities enough that I sank back into my chair.

"Trying to get rid of me?" At least my voice didn't sound close to tears like my tightened chest suggested releasing.

Malachi let out another long exhale. "No." He

moved his focus away again, shifting on his chair. "Yes." A soft snort accompanied a shake of his head. "Honestly, Isaac, I don't know."

I focused on the "no" answer, and warmth flooded through me with the understanding that we both bobbed in the ocean.

My threatening tears of hurt turned into ones of relief, but I choked them back. "I'm leaving in three weeks." I answered what I would do on the day I turned eighteen—no matter what.

He nodded, his attention once more returning to my face. Worry etched his brow. "Do you have any arrangements in place? A place to stay? A job?"

I might only be seventeen, but I wasn't a moron like Dad assumed. Heading out of state to chase my dreams with all my belongings in the back of my Camry was no plan.

"I have enough money saved up from mowing lawns the past four years that I won't need a full-time job for a couple months," I told Malachi what Dad didn't know, what he'd never considered asking. "But I have over a dozen applications in at retail and grocery stores. Two restaurants for a dishwasher position too."

He nodded. "And where will you sleep?"

"Until I have a job and can find a roommate, I'll be staying at the backpacker's hostel in midtown."

"It's a nice place. Clean. Safe." He grimaced like he'd said too much.

One of my eyebrows arched. "You've been there." I didn't bother raising my voice at the end to insinuate a question.

"Yes," he answered anyway, his lips immediately flatlining again.

"Want to talk about it?"

"No." He cleared his throat. "I know you don't think your parents love you—"

"Mom does. Dad doesn't."

Those blue eyes searched mine, and I didn't shield my expression like he did. Let him see what he would. We'd connected that first night by my parents' fire pit over both of us being gifts to our parents, prayed for by God. You'd think those who'd longed to hold a son of their own would treat them a little better though.

"He wants what's best for you," Malachi finally said.

"Sure as hell doesn't act like it." My chin tipped upward as I pushed away the stinging pain that always accompanied my reiteration over Dad loving his Bible, his God, more than he did me.

"He's worried for you."

"He doesn't know me."

"Have you offered him the chance?"

I held Malachi's stare for a few tense, silent moments. "Did *you* give your parents that chance?"

He tore his gaze off my face to his fingers still clenched atop his desk.

Guess not. Yet another thing he and I had in common.

I willed him to unclench his hands, round the desk, and touch me. Hold me. Allow us to offer each other what we both craved. Affection. Acceptance.

Maybe a climax or three.

"No, I never told them," he whispered rather than calling me out for turning the focus on him.

His answer was a confession as far as I was concerned, of who he was, *what* he was. But I wanted more. "Why not?"

"Because I grew up believing there was something wrong with me."

I could *feel* the connection between us, and by the way he peered at me without judgement in his eyes, I knew he did too.

No need for me to admit the truth of my insecurities, but I could steer our conversation to a different truth.

"Getting hard for another guy isn't wrong."

He swallowed, his Adam's apple bobbing. I imagined licking over it, tasting his skin.

My chub returned.

Malachi once more turned his attention to his hands like he couldn't bear to look at me. "It's a sin," he rasped.

"Yeah," I snorted, "according to a fairytale book written by a bunch of men who didn't know their assholes from their mouths—if they even existed at all."

He closed his eyes. "I believe the Word of God is true."

I sure as fuck didn't want to, but a part of me deep inside my soul feared it. If God *was*, then that meant He had allowed me to be formed with desires for the same sex. And yet He would reject me for living the life He'd supposedly blessed me with?

Talk about utter bullshit.

"So, you think we'll burn in hell for what we did." I didn't voice a question since Malachi thought the same as my dad.

"I'm sorry for my actions, Isaac. What I did was inappropriate. What happened between us was a mistake I've repented for."

I crossed my arms, my gaze narrowing as he lifted his head once more. The linking bond between us snapped back into place. "I sure as fuck haven't—and I never will. That was the hottest night of my life, and I can't stop thinking about it. Dreaming about it."

My dick agreed, swelling inside my boxers.

"I would appreciate if you wouldn't bring up what's been covered by the blood of the Lamb."

Words. All a bunch of repeated nonsense. Fucking bullshit. Having Bible terms tossed in my face only ever roused anger inside me to the point I seethed.

So much for that boner.

"The fuck, Malachi?" I scowled, hating that he'd deviated away from his straight shooting.

"He promised in the book of Ezekiel that He would cleanse us from our impurities."

I studied the man before me, looking for the peace and joy Dad's flock all sought after. "And has He given you that new heart, the new spirit He promised in the verse following that one?"

Pansy ass wouldn't even glance my way, couldn't be honest with himself.

Malachi would blindly choose his faith, his God, the words written by man that I'd been forced to memorize, over what brewed between us.

An ache spread through my chest, even as I pushed at the truth wanting to drown my heart.

"Tell me you aren't hard right now, Malachi." My voice wavered. "Tell me you don't want to shove your dick into my asshole and make me yours."

A shudder rippled over him as our gazes once more clashed. Lust, hot and thick, grew between us, the kind of evidence that couldn't be denied.

"I don't," he whispered.

"You're a goddamn liar," I shot back, my voice cracking as the pain beneath my breastbone sharpened. "Your eyes, the tension riding your shoulders says otherwise. Tell me you don't feel this." I motioned between us. "This...this energy, this *pull*. It's a damn craving that refuses to relent."

He held my stare but didn't answer.

"You're full of shit." I stood. "A fake ass hypocrite preaching about grace and acceptance." I snorted. "You need to give yourself some of both. Maybe it'll open your eyes to the truth of who and what you are."

I stormed out of his office, slamming his door shut behind me.

Thank fuck the door to Dad's office was closed. Last thing I needed was even more disappointment for failing to make a "friend."

Mom pulled into the parking lot as I stalked outside, and a lie about feeling sick got me her keys. She could catch a ride with Dad.

I went home, too torn up inside to write music, too angry to do anything but strip, curl up in my bed, and cry. I couldn't even rouse myself to pack a bag and get the hell out of there.

My cell dinged from my nightstand, and I swiped my forearm across my eyes while reaching for it.

Probably Mom checking up on me.

HAFYP: **You're right.**

I huffed a sarcastic laugh and replied to the hot as fuck youth pastor who'd never texted me before: **About wanting me or being a hypocrite?**

HAFYP: **About needing to give myself grace and acceptance. For denying who I am. But I still stand by what I believe, Isaac.**

In the Bible. In God who would damn me and

Malachi for what He'd allowed between us. I hoped
God wasn't real. Hoped He would prove Himself to
be nothing but a pack of lies.

Malachi texted two minutes later while I stewed
over the bullshit of a religion based on a God of love.

HAFYP: **I failed you in causing you to fall, and
I'm sorry. Please don't take off out of anger.**

How the fuck had he known I'd been thinking
about leaving early?

I didn't reply because I had nothing else to say to
the man who refused to acknowledge me in the way
I needed.

19

MALACHI

Hypocrite.

Isaac's accurate definition summed me up perfectly.

But he forgot to add liar. Unbeliever. Manipulator. And the list could go on. I was nothing but a filthy sinner. Unworthy of God's love.

I slid off my chair onto the office floor seconds after the door slammed shut behind Isaac and confessed to every single sin I could remember. For giving in to the temptation I'd lied about repenting for. For touching one of God's children—even if he was a man. For enjoying having him in my hands and not truly being sorry for it.

Tears streamed down my cheeks, and my knees ached by the time I finished—but I didn't feel cleansed.

My heart didn't feel new.

I still wanted Isaac with a deep-seated ache that threatened to break me.

Why didn't His promises hold true?

How long would He ask his children to have faith and to believe His plan without some sort of answer or guidance?

It didn't seem right—or fair.

Brian.

A headache spread between my temples as I recognized the tension taking control of my muscles over thoughts of my friend. I wanted to bare my teeth. Plant a fist into my office wall, smashing through drywall. Maybe hitting a stud would cause enough pain to keep me from going down the route that had led me off a path of righteousness five years earlier.

I struggled to breathe normally. Steadily.

Help me, please.

Refusing to let anger dictate my actions, I did what God would have me do. I confessed to Isaac and asked his forgiveness. But I couldn't bear to hear his voice. I took the coward's way out and texted.

Then when he didn't reply, I went on to beg him not to leave—but not just because I didn't want Pastor Bram to blame me for upsetting his son and being the cause of his running off.

I couldn't stand the idea of him going so far away. Admitting that to myself made me feel even more shitty.

Settling in Elkins had been a trial unlike any I'd faced before, and my old sinful nature battled with all I believed to be true.

Isaac never responded, and I hid out in my office like a chickenshit after I could hear the praise and worship team lead the congregation to start the service.

Stretched out on my office floor in a suit and tie, I dialed up Zeke, even though I knew he'd be in church.

"Hey," he surprisingly answered, breathless.

"Hello, Ezekiel," I tried for my usual teasing, but my voice fell flat.

"You okay?" Damn man was intuitive as hell and let my attempts to ruffle his feathers slide.

"No."

"Hold on a second." He muffled his cell, his low voice indistinct as he spoke to someone. A bit of static, like he brushed his cell against cloth, and he came back to me. "What's going on?"

"I fucked up, nothing makes sense, and my mind is seriously fucked up."

"What happened?"

"You got an hour?" I tried to joke again.

"Anything for you."

I quietly spilled the shit of Maine, not leaving anything out, hoping that confessing with my mouth would give me the peace He promised.

It didn't come to flood my soul, and my throat

tightened as Zeke remained silent for a few seconds once I finished my agonizing tale.

"Are you drawn to him because he reminds you of Brian?" he finally asked.

"No," I didn't hesitate to answer. "Isaac is different than Brian was. He's...more. Too much." I scratched beneath my tie, the buttons of my shirt snagging my fingernails. "Whatever this is between us, it's ten times more potent than anything I've felt before, Zeke. It's consuming. Inescapable.

"Why would God bring me to a place of temptation when all I've been trying to do is please Him? How could a God of love be so cruel?" Even as I asked the questions, guilt swept in to make my body want to sink through the floor, straight down into hell where I belonged.

Zeke didn't speak.

"Denying Isaac, the connection between us, makes me feel like I can't breathe," I choked out in a mere whisper. "Like I'm drowning. Being around him is life. Oxygen to starved lungs. I don't think I'll be able to stand him leaving—I can't be here when he goes."

"Then don't be."

I pinched the bridge of my nose, wanting to rant and rail on my friend for not offering me Godly counsel. "Give me Bible verses, Zeke. Give me truth. Words to live by."

"I don't have the answers."

I opened my eyes and stared, noticing of a small water leak stain in the textured ceiling. "Isn't the Bible supposed to have all the answers?"

"Supposed to."

That didn't sound like my confident friend. At all.

"What's going on, Zeke?"

He let out a heavy exhale, taking too long to respond. My own issues faded enough from my mind that I grew concerned for him. "It's a story for another time, but suffice to say that pre-marriage counseling young couples is making me question my own faith."

"How so?"

"Like I said—story for another time."

"Fine." I sat back up, one arm resting over my drawn-up knees. "So, forget the Bible and our faith for a minute. What advice have you got for me?"

"We can't just set those things aside," Zeke tried to reason, and I closed my eyes again. "Going with your guts, your heart, will put Isaac beneath you, but it'll also end with you losing your job and the chance to ever influence teenagers in a church setting again."

That last bit of truth hit hard, especially since I thought God had called me to work with teens. I'd wanted to do His will in honor of my parents for their years of sacrifice and love for me.

Was allowing myself to give in to the unholy craving for Isaac worth eternal damnation?

Considering I didn't know exactly what hell consisted of, I wondered.

Would pursuing the feelings inside me, the possibility of...perhaps love, give my soul what it longed for, what God hadn't been able to fill?

That question haunted me for the next half hour after I'd hung up with Zeke, and when Pastor Bram came looking for me after the service, I still didn't have any answers.

He eyed me still sitting on my floor. "Are you okay, Malachi?"

"Yeah." My voice sounded like I'd swallowed a bag full of crushed glass.

"Annabelle said Isaac went home feeling sick."

"He did?" I couldn't bring myself to look at my pastor.

"Did something happen?"

Nothing physical, thank God.

"No," I answered, scrubbing a hand down over my face, knowing I needed to lie for both our sakes. "I've just been on my knees for your son."

The filthy image that flashed through my head made me want to groan.

Pastor Bram let out a sigh. "I guess girding your loins hasn't helped."

Loins. Damnit.

I choked on a cough/laugh, sure I was losing my goddamn mind. "He's a handful."

Shit.

My pastor came fully into my office, offering to help me to my feet. I accepted, my thoughts filled with self-loathing to the point my stomach twisted.

"I know I just started here, but to be honest...I'm feeling overwhelmed," I admitted what I could.

"Do you need a few days off?"

"I hate asking, but it would probably be for the best."

No trace of anger or annoyance lined his forehead when I finally lifted my head. Pastor Bram smiled. "I know just the place, but it won't be available until three weeks from now."

Three weeks. The weekend Isaac turned eighteen and would leave—if he hadn't already.

"That would actually be perfect," I said, forcing a smile.

"You can hang in until then?" Pastor Bram clasped my shoulder, and I nodded. "Good, because the cottage we co-own up on Lake Wallenpaupack isn't rented that weekend. It's a perfect escape and all yours if you want."

"Thank you, and yes," I didn't hesitate to answer.

"It's settled, then." His smile widened. "Now come out and show your face as the congregation leaves. There were lots of wondering glances at your empty chair during service."

"I'm sorry."

"It's okay." He chuckled as I followed him out my office door. "The younger ladies all listened to my sermon for a change. I'm guessing God had something for me to say to one of them that wouldn't have heard were you sitting behind me in full view."

Oh, how easily he accepted the possibilities of God's plan.

Had he known why I'd been absent, he wouldn't have been so understanding.

20

ISAAC

A week dragged past, raining damn near every day.

I went to the movies with Chris and Tyler without my parents knowledge. Seeing as how the ways of the world were of the devil, Hollywood was a no-no. But when had I ever listened?

Chris brought along a bag of weed, and I smoked my first joint later that night, out in the deep, water-logged woods.

And fuck, did I feel fine.

Relaxed.

Tyler claimed smoking weed always gave him such clarity, like he could figure out the cares of the world.

I ended up numb and didn't complain, just simply chowed down on fast food fries and a milkshake we snagged from a drive-through on the way back to my house.

The guys dropped me off, even though I still floated high as shit.

Thank fuck my parents went to bed and trusted me with a twelve o'clock curfew.

Neither sat up waiting for me since I'd gone out with kids from the youth group to hang out at Dunks and talk about Jesus over coffee and donuts.

Lies.

I snuck up to my bed, grinning like an idiot.

Stripped bare, I slid between my sheets, thinking I'd never felt such a soft bed.

Instead of lying there and agonizing over Malachi and how my angry thoughts toward him didn't match up with my lustful desires like I'd been doing for what seemed like forever, I passed the fuck out.

The next morning, I called up Chris and talked him into selling me some pot of my own.

He had me covered.

———

I cooked up another lie about having an upset stomach to skip church that Sunday. Mom tucked me back into bed before leaving. Dad checked in on me after church, stern and disappointed as always.

But I didn't give a shit. I didn't have to see Malachi.

Wednesday rolled around, and I knew Dad wouldn't let me get away with missing out on two services in a row.

I texted Chris and had him meet me out behind the school for a quick smoke. The nerves I'd felt racing over my skin at seeing the old truck in the parking lot faded more with every hit of the sweet burn filling my lungs.

We ended up giggling like a couple of kids over... well, shit I couldn't even remember.

"My eyes red?" I asked him as we rounded the school for the gymnasium doors.

"Anyone asks, just say it's allergies. Works every time."

"Hey, I'm sorry about the whole Maine thing." I brought up what we hadn't discussed sober.

"I heard your whistle," Chris said with a shrug. "Just didn't feel like taking my hands off of Sara's tits. They're fucking fantastic."

"Have you two..."

"She won't let me fuck her, but we're hanging out. I'll talk her into it eventually."

"What?" I barked a laugh. "You have magic mojo or some shit that gets you into a girl's pants?"

Chris laughed too. "Nah, but that girl gives me heart eyes. She wants me. Lets me have a little more whenever we have a few minutes alone. It's only a matter of time."

"And circumstance," I said, remembering having Malachi all to myself that night in Maine.

"Yeah, that." Chris pulled open the gym's door. "Tough when you've got religious parents breathing down your damn neck."

"Talk about truth," I muttered, following on his heels, keeping my focus on the floor so I wouldn't have to see Malachi. I could feel him, though. Heat sizzled my skin, and I wanted to laugh my ass off for some reason.

Fucking high—felt fucking great.

Grinning, I sprawled into the chair beside Chris, and we whispered a bit until Malachi called our meeting to order. I couldn't focus on what he said, not that I ever truly did, but I caught words here and there.

God's plan.

His leading.

Something about His having our best interest at heart.

I snorted at that one. Finally glancing up, I caught Malachi's glare. I grinned.

He blinked.

Turned away and kept talking.

More Bible verse bullshit, blah, blah, blah.

Chris leaned over my way, starting to rhyme with words Malachi used.

Word. Turd.

Heart. Fart.

Typical guy shit, but they were the funniest rhymes I'd ever heard. I barked out a laugh, fighting to act sober when both Malachi and Miss Jennifer frowned our way.

The second time Chris had me bursting out, Malachi stopped talking altogether and faced us.

"Both of you—out in the hallway. Now."

My blood raced, remembering the last time he'd taken me from the youth circle, but with Chris tagging along, I knew there wouldn't be a visit to the janitor's closet.

We both snickered, stepping into the hallway, Malachi on my ass.

Not on my ass literally...unfortunately.

"Damn," I muttered, imagining that very thing.

Miss Jennifer's voice lifted in song, but the slam of the gym door cut her off.

"I don't appreciate the disruptions tonight, boys."

Chris and I pulled up and turned to face our youth pastor.

Lips in a thin line, eyes hard, he glanced between the two of us. Thank fuck Chris was flying like a kite too or he probably would have felt the energy zapping and tingling across my skin.

I held Malachi's stare.

His gaze narrowed. "Are you high?"

Chris giggled, and I fought to keep my lips from curving. "Nope." I popped the P.

Malachi's shoulders dropped, and his glare morphed into something I was well acquainted with —disappointment.

"I'm outta here." I spun and strode away before he could start spouting off bullshit about making better choices and acting like a child of God since others looked up to me as the pastor's son.

"Isaac!"

I ignored Malachi and pushed open the door, letting myself outside to blow off some steam.

He didn't follow me, and I couldn't decide if I was happy or pissed while sulking on a swing in the play area, waiting for church to end.

Wednesday night service let out ten minutes later, and Dad drove us home. I slouched in the back while he and Mom discussed the message he'd preached.

The second we got to the house, I shut myself in my room, needing a joint, but I didn't have the balls to smoke until Mom and Dad went to bed.

I laid in my bed, fully clothed, hating the feeling of coming back down to reality.

"Isaac?" Dad knocked and opened my door without waiting for me to tell him he could enter. The guy didn't give two shits about privacy when it came to his household.

Thank fuck I hadn't been jerking off.

His brow furrowed as he walked in, Mom on his heels. Concern etched her face, and the wringing hands at her front let me know shit was about to hit the fan.

"I just talked to Malachi," Dad said, his voice stern.

Yeah, I could imagine he had.

"Have you been smoking pot?"

The fucker ratted me out.

"Nope," I lied.

"Sit up."

I did as Dad commanded, holding in my annoyed sigh that would only make shit ten times worse.

"Your eyes are bloodshot."

"Allergies."

"You've never had allergies before."

I shrugged, taking more interest in the torn denim over my knee. "People develop allergies later in life."

"You're no longer allowed to be friends with Chris."

That earned Dad a steady gaze. "What?"

"He's a bad influence."

I glanced at Mom, but she wouldn't meet my eyes.

"He got that girl pregnant two years ago," Dad continued, shoulders back and chin lifted while looking at me, taking his position of authority in the household damn seriously.

"And he repented," I reminded Dad. "Publicly from the pulpit like you and his parents thought best."

"Still." Dad's lips thinned.

"Why would you bring up the past that's been covered by the blood?" I couldn't help but ask, my own brow furrowing to match his. "Who are you to uncover Chris's sins?"

"I'm the father of an impressionable young man who doesn't know how to make right decisions!" His voice shook, his dark eyes growing stormy.

I would have been smarter to shut my damn mouth, but I didn't give a shit that he'd probably try to take the rod to me like the Bible commanded.

"Well, I'm sorry I can't be the Isaac of your precious Word," I half-spat, standing to my feet. "And I'm sorry I can't be the perfect son you hoped and prayed for."

"Isaac—"

"You don't listen to a word I say," I cut Dad off, the bullshit of my circumstances...of Malachi's disappointment in me rousing to an ugly brew of toxicity in my gut. "You couldn't care less about what I think or feel."

"That's not true," Mom started, but I wasn't done.

"Nothing I say is good enough. Holy enough. All

you care about is your Bible and the flock God called you to lead."

"Isaac—"

"No!" I hollered at Dad, my hands fisted at my sides. "If you gave me even a quarter of the time you give to your God, your congregation—hell, an eighth of the time you spend readying to preach, you'd—"

"Enough!" Dad barked and started toward me, his hand lifting.

I held my chin high—waiting for him to award me with a reason to escape early.

Mom burst into tears. "Bram!"

Her cry halted Dad's feet, and we glared at one another across the distance.

"I want you out," Dad bit the words.

"No!" Mom sobbed and grabbed hold of his hand. "Bram, please!"

"The day you turn eighteen," he continued, ignoring Mom, "you're on your own. We have offered you everything we could—life, a home..."

I barely stifled my snort when he didn't continue on with the words of unconditional love like a parent should. "Don't worry," I promised, "I'll be gone the second midnight passes."

A muscle jumped in Dad's jaw, and he spun, leaving me and Mom alone.

Tears coursed down her cheeks, and my shoulders slumped.

"I'm sorry—"

"No." She moved in close, grasping my face, her eyes wet. "I love you. Always. No matter what."

What if Dad made her choose between him and I? Telling them my sexual orientation would definitely put her in that position, but I couldn't do that to the one person who'd tried to love me the best she could.

"I'm still going."

Another tear slid down her cheek. "I know."

"There's nothing here for me, Mom," I choked out, hating the thickness wanting to take away my voice. "You've done your best—and I appreciate that—but this isn't my home anymore."

Her lower lip trembled as she nodded. "You need to find your own way." She inhaled a shuddered sigh. "I'll have to trust God to see you through."

I pulled Mom into my arms, wishing I could tell her the truth about who I was to her God and what I thought of Him.

Two weeks.

I could put up with Dad's shit.

For Mom.

21

MALACHI

Isaac ignored me again.

I did the same with him, and I hurt because of it.

Even more, I hated how he appeared whenever I allowed myself a peek in his direction. He sat slouched at youth group, keeping to himself like he'd done when I'd first arrived.

Pastor Bram informed me about their fallout after I'd told him about Isaac's behavior, one thing I regretted even though his disrespect had pissed me off. Pastor Bram assured me with obvious displeasure in his voice that I only had to deal with his rebellious son for a little while longer.

That Isaac was a disappointment to him reaffirmed strongly in my heart.

Was it any wonder Isaac behaved the way he did? Why didn't he take off early for Nashville like I felt sure he wanted to? And why did I feel the need to talk to him, to make things right between us? I'd have been better off leaving him alone, allowing him his emotions, thoughts, and distance which would separate us for good.

I couldn't.

If nothing else, it was my responsibility to share my story and maybe influence his future decisions.

Perhaps that was why God had led me to Elkins.

Hinging my thoughts on that idea, I went looking for Isaac the day before I planned to head to the Van Dusen's camp on Lake Wallenpaupack. I drove around their neighborhood since he did yard work, both windows down and ears straining for the sounds of a mower.

Isaac labored beneath the hot sun, shirtless and sweating, two blocks from home. Old jean shorts hung low on his hips.

"Shit," I muttered, the ruckus from the small engine of his mower drowning out my curse.

My heart sped as I pulled to the curb in front of the neighbor's house, studying how his legs and backside flexed with every step away from me. Lust kicked in like it always did whenever I filled my eyes with Isaac's lithe body and smooth skin.

I couldn't find repentance in my heart for the curse or the craving that wanted to dictate my actions.

Teeth clenched and unable to pray for strength, I

put my dad's old truck into park, shut off the ignition, and sat.

Watching.

Waiting for him to make the turn, to glance up and see me.

Ten agonizing seconds passed before he came into profile, his focus on the grass and the path he intended to take.

Look at me.

As though hearing my thought, Isaac stopped, and his head snapped up, gaze landing on Dad's truck.

I didn't know if he could see me through the windshield, but my breath still caught and time paused for a moment. My mouth salivated for a taste of the sweat on his face. Fingers itched to peel the jean shorts down over his lean hips. Dick throbbed to fill him over and over until we both found release.

"Fuck." I rubbed a hand over my face, and he cut the engine, leaving the air around me silent.

His shoulders rose like he took a fortifying breath, and he walked my way. Steps steady. Chin raised. Like he faced war—and was damn ready for it.

My skin came alive the closer he got, and my pulse raced once I could make out the green in his hazel eyes.

He stood by my rolled down window, and I filled my lungs, dragging in the scent of sweat and soap.

"Can we talk?" I croaked out, realizing I held the steering wheel in a death grip.

Isaac glanced over at the yard he'd been mowing. "Give me a few minutes to finish up."

"Yeah. Okay." I nodded, feeling like a bumbling idiot, and he held my gaze for a few more seconds before heading to work.

His backside drew my focus, and I cursed, sure he put a little extra sway in his step to drive me insane.

Balls and jaw aching, I stared like a pervert while he finished the final three rows of the lawn. He pushed the mower down the sidewalk toward where I waited, his shirt he'd retrieved from the front porch thrown over one shoulder.

Heat waves rose off the blacktop, infiltrating the cab of Dad's truck. Without any moving wind, we would roast talking inside.

I hopped from the cab, knowing that at four in the afternoon he had to be done for the day. "All set?"

"Yeah." He glanced down the road toward home.

"Can I give you a ride?" I offered, rounding the back of the truck.

"Yeah. Sure."

I put down the tailgate, and we lifted the mower together on either side, rolling it into the back.

The second he climbed into the truck, I rubbed

my palms against my own shorts, trying to rid them of dampness from sweat and nerves alike.

"Here." I grabbed one of the cold bottles of water I'd brought from home and handed it over.

Starting up the truck, I eyed him in my periphery. He was sucking down the cold liquid, his Adam's apple bobbing. A droplet of salty sweat trailed from his temple down his neck.

I swallowed my groan along with a flood of drool and faced forward before driving away from the curb.

"Thanks," he said, breathless after emptying the water bottle in one chug.

"Hot as hell out there."

"Yeah."

"You're leaving in two days."

Isaac didn't bother responding since I hadn't asked a question.

"I-I hoped to talk to you before you did."

"So talk," he said, his words snipped.

"I'm sorry for ratting you out to your dad."

"Yeah—thanks for that."

"It's my duty as your youth pastor. I want what's best for you—"

"Spare me the bullshit, Malachi."

Lips clamped, I nodded. There would be no making of amends which was probably for the best no matter how much I'd hoped to at least be friends.

The wind whipped through the cab as I drove past his house, but I still sweated inside my T-shirt.

"Where are we going?"

"Someplace quiet."

Tension rose between us at the suggestion we would be alone. Private. Perhaps even in seclusion.

I couldn't allow the temptation.

Two minutes later, I pulled alongside the pines crowding the town park. Kids played on the swings and climbing apparatuses, their laughter and shrieks taking over the silence between us as I shut down the engine.

"Come on." I squeaked the door open and climbed out.

Isaac did the same and tugged his shirt on overhead.

I breathed a bit easier at not having to talk to him with all that skin I wanted to explore on display.

We settled beneath an oak tree a good fifty feet away from the nearest parent watching over the play area.

"I was ten when I realized I liked boys," I started off our conversation without any bullshit. "No women ever caught my attention, and none ever will."

Isaac sat silent, his arms draped over his pulled-up knees.

"I went to Nashville out of rebellion to God," I continued after stating the truth Isaac already knew about my sexuality. "I wanted to prove myself and made all kinds of mistakes that left me feeling empty. The first was being naive enough to believe a big wig in the industry had fallen for me. He promised me a record deal in exchange for my virginity."

My stomach heaved, but I continued before Isaac could interrupt the shit I needed to spew.

"And I gave it to him, only to be laughed at and tossed out his door an hour later. After that, I spent years making bad choices that led to depression and more heartache. The thought of you facing the same thing..." I grimaced as my stomach rolled. Again. "I wish I could keep you from experiencing the hell I did, Isaac. All I can do is beg you to stay in the Word. Pray. Ask God for guidance."

I could feel Isaac's stare on my face but couldn't look at him. Sitting that close, within touching distance, and peering into his eyes would prove my undoing.

"While my mom lay on her deathbed, I decided to rededicate my life to God, thinking of the truth I'd been raised in." I pushed on telling my story in the hopes my ending would encourage him toward the right path. "I lived in the hype, the emotionalism all through college, my best friend Zeke being the one to help me keep my head above water. After graduation and my dad's death last summer, I was faced with life on my own, without guidance from a parent. I decided to change the scenery and start over with a new beginning."

"That's what led you here."

"Yes."

I stared at the little kids running around, seeing but not processing their actions beyond movement.

"It's not sin if you don't act on it," I whispered, hoping like hell Isaac would listen.

"I *want* to act on it."

Hell. I closed my eyes, teeth clenched. He hadn't heard a damn word I'd said.

"More than anything," Isaac said, "I want a taste of the forbidden."

"It's an addictive drug," I choked out, "one that will do nothing but cause harm."

"You know that from experience." Isaac didn't ask a question, but I nodded all the same, needing to voice what I'd lived through—for his sake.

"Yes." I swallowed hard, finally forcing myself to meet Isaac's stare. Goosebumps rose on my skin, the electric current between us zapping with undeniable pulses. "And because of our sins, God took him from me."

Isaac's eyes stated I spewed nonsense, but I drove onward before he could deny what I knew to be truth, what my guilt still held over my head.

"In high school, I fell in love with the new boy in town." My voice wavered, so I tore my focus off of

Isaac's face in order to finish. "He was gay too. My first kiss—my first hand job. Blowjob."

I cleared my throat and pulled up my knees like Isaac did to lace my shaking fingers together at the front of my shins. "I instigated, and he followed me like a lamb to the slaughter. We hid our relationship for three years. The day after graduation, he lost control of his car and hit a tree head on. Brian died on impact."

Swallowing hard, I pushed away the hurt that had faded over the years but still stung like a bitch, the feelings of remorse as raw as they'd been at eighteen.

"I'm the one who led Brian into sin, and he's dead because of it."

Isaac snorted, stretched his legs out, and leaned back on his hands, removing himself from my from periphery. "My dad's God is supposed to be love—is that showing love? Taking away life for breaking a book's rule? I'm calling bullshit."

His matter-of-fact statement left me without words. The deepest part of me longed to believe as he did, what I'd told myself all those years in Nashville.

Help me.

The silent prayer rose in my head on its own, and I clung to the image in my mind of the Holy Spirit interceding on my behalf before the throne of God.

"I wanted to think the same," I finally managed

to speak, clinging to my faith to keep from floundering. "It's why I went to Nashville. It had been Brian's dream first, and I felt I owed his memory the chance to fulfill what we'd planned to do. We wrote music together. Sang duets in church. It was beautiful. *We* were beautiful."

"You still love him."

I considered Isaac's statement and pondered the ache in my chest I experienced whenever thinking about Brian. "A part of me always will, yes. But he's gone—he's not my future." I turned to catch Isaac's gaze. "I don't want you to hurt like I did, Isaac."

"I have to live my life."

I nodded since my tight throat kept me from speaking.

"It's one thing to hear of mistakes people have made," Isaac went on, "it's another thing to live them yourself. They don't always have to be regrets either. Sometimes they're the only circumstances that can make a stubborn person stronger."

The kid was too much…

"I have to make my own choices, my own mistakes," he continued giving me his truth. "And in the end, if I see blinding white light after breathing my last, I'll believe."

"At that point, it'll be too late."

"I don't give a shit. If God is the narcissistic prick the Bible makes Him out to be, then I'd rather burn in hell."

A fissure cracked through my heart. There would be no changing his mind, his plans.

"And until it's your time?" I asked quietly, needing something to imagine once he left.

"I'll love and accept others like Dad preaches from his pulpit but doesn't live."

22

ISAAC

Malachi stood after my declaration on how I planned to move forward, and I followed him back to his perfectly sexy truck. Our silence stretched throughout the ride home.

He helped me unload the lawnmower, and we both stood awkwardly, my hands clutching the old metal handle, his fisted at his sides.

"Your dad offered me use of your camp for the weekend, and I'm leaving in the morning."

I studied Malachi's profile as he glanced over to my parents' house. He'd been unable to hold my gaze for more than five seconds for weeks. "So this is goodbye."

Malachi swallowed and nodded.

Aching pain raced through my chest, but I lifted my chin and shoved my hand toward him even though I'd rather have grabbed him and kissed his mouth.

He eyed my shaking offer and let out a slow exhale before accepting.

Sweaty palms, grasping fingers. Clasping tight to soak in the ripple of want between us.

"Take care of yourself," he whispered, finally lifting his focus to my face.

My eyes stung at the troubled emotion in his, and I nodded, even though I wanted to beg *him* to take care of me. Show me everything I'd dreamed about. Craved. Exactly as his blue orbs suggested he longed for as well.

"I'll be praying for you."

My throat was too tight to tell him not to bother.

Malachi pulled his hand from mine and turned away, his shoulders hitched up. Choosing his God rather than the real, flesh and blood man who would worship at his feet given the chance.

Tension continued to radiate between us until he drove off without looking back, tearing my heart right down its center.

I swiped at my wet eyes the second the old truck disappeared from sight, filled my lungs, and trudged toward the shed out back to put the mower away, every step heavy. Every breath shallow. Every heartbeat painful.

Sleep wouldn't come that night, and my entire last

day as a seventeen-year-old was spent the same way as the one before. Sweat covered, driven to make every last dollar before I left for Nashville the next morning.

But rather than focusing on the excitement of escape—freedom—my feet dragged, my stride slow, like slugging through cement. My chest continued to ache, and each time I replayed Malachi driving away from me, my eyes stung.

The day's work lasted longer than the one before, and until I finished, I just wanted to curl up in bed and cry like a pansy. But I had shit to do. It took another hour to finish packing up my things and loading them into the car.

My Camry was gassed up and ready to roll with the sunrise.

One clean outfit and my bathroom bag remained in my room for morning.

We sat down to a late dinner, our final one as a family that from the outside appeared blessed. Godly and whole. Mom barely touched her food, her fork scraping as she pushed it around on her plate.

Dad ate as though unaffected, at ease because he trusted his God.

My knee bounced beneath the table even though my heart sat heavy in my chest.

Freedom meant leaving Malachi behind, and while I wanted the first, I craved the second just as badly.

"I wish you would reconsider and choose God's will for your life."

I glanced up at Dad who'd finished and placed his fork and knife upside down on his cleared plate. He always spoke as if he was privy to God's will for people's lives. But I was done being manipulated and shoved down a path I didn't want.

"I'm heading south in the morning," I told him, my tone firm.

Disappointment—big surprise—flashed in his eyes, only serving to ramp up my resolve. "Nashville can't possibly be the Lord's calling."

I'd had about enough of his bullshit and didn't bother hiding that truth from my eyes as I frowned. "And since when do you know the mind of your God?"

"*My* God?"

"Yes, *yours*," I tossed back, pushing my plate away since I'd had enough. "You stand up on that platform in church like you're some...some God-*sent* prophet, spouting off commandments about love and acceptance, when all I've ever gotten from you is correction and discipline."

"Please, Isaac, it's your last night with us," Mom said, her voice wavering. "Don't do this."

"Do what, Mom? Challenge what's been hammered into my brain since I was a kid, only to never see it in action?"

"That's enough, Isaac," Dad snapped.

I glared at him, his attempts to control me to the last minute raising my hackles. Tension made me stiffen in the chair, my hands fisting on my lap "No, it's not. *I've* had enough—of your hypocrisy and having to live a lie because telling you who I really am would only cause even more disappointment and damnation."

"What are you talking about?" Mom asked quietly while Dad and I held a staring contest.

"I'm. Gay." I bit the words out.

Mom gasped.

Surprise—then disgust—clouded Dad's eyes and furrowed his brow. "Get out," he whispered harshly, with more venom than any snake.

I shoved back my chair, toppling it over in a rush of adrenaline.

"Isaac!"

I ignored Mom and hurried up to my bedroom, her cries and Dad's rantings about me being an abomination, a pervert, reaching me upstairs. My legs shook, and my stomach clenched up tight as I grabbed the last bag, stuffing my bathroom things into it.

My cell sat on the bed stand, and I slid it into my back pocket. Without glancing around my childhood bedroom, I took my bag and strode down the stairs.

Mom still cried in the kitchen.

"No, Annabelle," Dad hissed. "I won't have that

—that unholy *creature* in this house a minute longer!"

For the first time, I hoped there really was a hell.

And I hoped Dad burned there for eternity.

The front door slammed shut behind me, and I beelined toward my car, adrenaline rushing, my entire body trembling.

A few hours earlier than I'd planned to leave, but I'd claim my freedom from that awful man all the same.

What father called his son such hurtful, hateful things? What happened to all those teachings about loving the sinner while hating the sin? Dad was only capable of showing hate—toward his own damn son. My chest tightened, but I gritted my teeth over my new truth.

I'm no longer his son.

I hopped in my car without an ounce of regret and tore out of the driveway, the tires squealing. I didn't even spare the house a glance in my rearview mirror.

At the crossroads, I pulled up to the stop sign, my entire body still trembling. The highway leading to Nashville lay straight ahead, the lake house to my left.

My dreams told me to take off toward Tennessee, to live my life and make those choices for myself. However, my heart, my gut turned my gaze east, a desperate longing to prove Malachi was nothing like my dad rushing through me.

Too many unspoken things remained between us. Too much hurt and anger sat in the back of my mind.

Moving on would be difficult without closure, and I couldn't stand the thought of not putting the issue of Malachi Foley to rest before starting my new life.

He might not want to be a part of my future, but I needed to hear those words clearly from his mouth before leaving. I needed to hear for myself that I hadn't been wrong about him, that he wasn't a true hypocrite at heart.

I couldn't go on believing he'd been fashioned from the same cloth as Bram Van Dusen.

I stomped on the gas and yanked the wheel toward my left, fishtailing my car.

My pulse thrummed, beating loudly in my ears. My dick chubbed in the hopes he would have me. My mind raced at the possibility of a new beginning —with him.

Steeling myself for disappointment, I sped up the highway, ready to put my fate in Malachi's hands.

23

———

MALACHI

I spent the entire afternoon sitting on the dock down by the lake, simply being. Diving into the cold depths when the sun and heat became too much.

No office phone, no questioning teenagers, and no duties other than trying to figure out my head, my heart, clattered for my attention. Evaluating my emotions wasn't a simple task, but I forced myself to think on them rather than deny. I recognized pain. Disappointment and what seemed like crushing loss.

No joy filled me at having the space, the break I thought I'd needed.

I sipped my third beer while grilling a steak, having repented prior to purchasing the six-pack I'd bought for over the weekend. No guilt rested on my shoulders while I ate my dinner outside. The sun sank, creating a rainbow of color across the sky, but I couldn't find beauty in God's creation. Not even the birds tweeting an early goodnight gave me happiness.

Breathing didn't come as easily as I'd hoped. My chest still ached, the hollowness inside me a constant.

Are You real? I gave up my dream to follow You, trusted You to guide my path. I've held onto my faith, stumbling blindly through the darkness...

A chittering squirrel drew my attention off the inward thoughts, and I watched as two of them scampered up and around a pine tree beside the Van Dusens' cabin.

The small, two-bedroom cottage sat less than fifty yards from the water's edge. Quaint. Quiet.

A good place to rest.

If only I'd been able to find some for my mind.

Letting out a heavy exhale, I gathered up my dinner things and made my way inside.

Minutes later, I stood beneath the shower's hot spray, ridding my skin of the lake's scent. The temptation to take myself in hand and jerk off to thoughts of Isaac battled with the heaviness in my heart.

The loss of him...it hurt like Brian's death had. Hell, it hurt worse, seeming to crush my heart where it lay beating by instinct alone.

A shiver licked over my skin, pebbling my arms, even though heat enveloped me.

I lifted my eyes to the fogged glass.

Someone stood in the bathroom's opened doorway.

Isaac.

I could feel the energy from him feeding my soul, and a rush of adrenaline—excitement and fear combined—made my knees weak. Could he see me through the glass better than I could him? Did he notice how my dick went from lax to interested within seconds?

Shutting off the water, my mind raced over what to do. Why he would be there. What he hoped to accomplish by putting us in a private situation.

It didn't take a single brain cell to guess.

I grabbed the towel I'd slung over the shower wall and wrapped it around my waist before pushing the glass door outward.

It swung, bringing Isaac into sight.

His brow was furrowed, eyes full of anxiety. Shoulders hitched with tension. Hands fisted at his sides.

"Isaac?" I asked, stepping out of the shower and onto the mat, dripping water everywhere.

"I told them."

It took me a second to process his words—and the blood drained from my face, my dick drooping as fast as it'd risen for him. "What?" I rasped out.

"My parents. I told them I'm gay."

My breath left in a rush, and I closed my eyes briefly, thankful he hadn't confessed to our sins.

"Are you going to ask me what they said that hurt more than your rejection or thank me for not getting you fired?"

Shit.

I swallowed hard at his glinting glare. How well he knew me...a seventeen-year-old kid I'd met mere months earlier. "What did he say to you?" I asked, knowing it would have been Bram rather than Annabelle who'd inflicted this emotional pain.

"He ordered me to get out." Isaac lifted his chin.

"What did he say to you, Isaac?" I asked again, taking two steps closer, wanting to offer comfort for the hurt etched in his eyes, the kind of crushing sorrow I couldn't bear the thought of him carrying.

"He c-called me an unholy creature. A p-pervert." His Adam's apple bobbed as he swallowed. "An abomination."

"Asshole," I hissed and swiped my palm down over my face to rid it of dripping water. "Damn him."

"To hell," Isaac stated, his tone finding its sternness again. "For eternity."

Lips in a thin line, I glanced down over him, anger and lust a bitter brew in my guts. He was perfectly trim. Perfectly formed. Perfectly beautiful in his ripped jeans and scuffed black Vans.

"You're leaving."

"The car's packed, but I had to see you first."

"I'm sorry, Isaac."

"Is that your way of telling me to get out?"

I glanced around the bathroom, my emotions tangled, my thoughts and truth at war. "I feel like your final months at home would have been easier if I'd never come to Elkins."

"I wouldn't change a goddamn thing." Isaac stepped in close, an arm's reach away, his hazel eyes peering into mine with intent. Lustful. Hopeful. "I've wanted you from the moment I saw you at the bottom of the stairs. You brought the dead part inside of me alive. Gave me something to cling to rather than the depression always hanging over my head."

His words radiated through me, so damn similar to my own emotions that my throat tightened. "We can't," I whispered rather than admitting I felt the same.

"We actually can."

"It's a sin."

Isaac stepped closer, laying his palm on my chest —damn near burning me and snagging my breath. "If that's what you believe this is, then I want to sin."

"You know I believe it."

"Well, I think you need to start using this—" he grabbed my dick "—instead of your head."

Fuck.

I hissed out an exhale as he squeezed and fondled my length to full life. "Isaac," I croaked, fighting my flesh and its lustful craving by fisting my hands at my sides.

"Hmm?" He studied my lower lip as I tried to lick moisture back to its dry flesh. One squeeze of my balls, and I lost my mind.

"Goddamnit." I grabbed hold of his head and smashed my lips to his, driving him backward until he hit the doorjamb.

"Ung," he groaned, giving me access to the sweet and spicy wetness of his mouth, the warmth inside. Hungry tongues dueled in a primal dance, and I ground my dick against his hand.

He grasped at my towel—it fell to the floor—his hot flesh replacing cotton to rub over my burning skin.

"Oh fuck," I groaned across his lips, panting. Urgency dictated, and I released his head, fumbling with his jeans' button.

"Hurry," Isaac whispered as I pulled back to see what I was doing.

Button.

Zipper.

Shove the jeans down to his ankles.

His gorgeous dick sprang upward into my hands. Hard and leaking—for me.

"Fuck yes." I dropped to my knees to the cool tile without a thought beyond tasting him. Smearing his pre-cum over my lips and licking them clean.

"Shit...fucking hell..."

My mouth closed over his swollen head, his saltiness coating my tongue. "Mmm," I hummed around him, taking him deep.

A thump accompanied his groan, and I glanced up to find his head tipped back against the doorjamb. Lips parted, he panted, and I buried my face into his groin, swallowing around his girth.

"Holy...f-fuck..."

His hips moved with me, giving me what I wanted—his dick shoved down my throat.

Shudders rippled through him, whimpers and gasps filling my ears and making me hard as granite.

I pulled off and shoved my tongue into his slit, searching for more of his salty precum.

"Fuck." He dropped his chin, eyelids fluttering open. Hazel eyes hazed with lust peered down at me.

The youth pastor on his knees, worshiping his cock.

Guilt rose to choke me, but I took him deep again, holding his stare.

Need this.

Need him.

Just this once.

I fondled his tight sack, my fingertip sliding over his perineum.

"Yes—please touch me, Malachi." He licked his lips, his hands finding the sides of my head to hold on tight. "Please. Please..."

He widened his stance, allowing me free access

—and I took it, brushing the pad of my fingertip over his asshole.

"Oh God." His head hit the doorjamb again.

I rubbed, sucked, and swallowed around his length, all the while watching the twitches on his expressive face, the throes of passion overtaking him and parting his pouty lips.

Give it to me.

As though hearing my thoughts, Isaac opened his eyes. Met my gaze again—and came without warning, shooting spurts of thickness into my throat.

"Ung..." He groaned, thrust, gulped, and cursed, and my dick leaked precum onto the bathroom floor between my knees. "Holy f-fucking hell, Malachi," he rasped in a spine-tingling tone.

I sucked every last drop from his slit and sat back, my hands falling to my thighs.

Our gazes held, our pants echoing in the small room.

"Another first." A smirk curled the corner of his lips as he sagged against the wall, breathless. He glanced down at my aching dick I refrained from touching. "Want to take more?"

The fuck are you doing?

I closed my eyes, disgust over my weakness rising up like bile to burn the back of my throat. Grabbing my fallen towel, I stood and covered myself. "I'm sorry—"

"Don't you fucking dare." Isaac shoved his dick

back into his jeans while I wrapped the towel around my waist with shaking hands.

"You can't—"

"Don't throw me out." His cracking voice made me pause, and I forced myself to look him in the eyes.

Pain filled their depths, the kind that assured me of the hurt Bram had inflicted. My heart ached for him even more than my balls did for release. Sending him away would be beyond cruel, and I couldn't bear to shred his heart more than his dad had already.

I let out a heavy exhale, knowing the temptation I faced in taking pity on the one my entire body longed for. "You can stay in the second bedroom tonight."

His smooth jaw clenched, and he turned without another word.

Once locked in the master bedroom, I leaned against the door and closed my eyes. While regret filled me over my actions, I had zero desire to get on my knees to beg for God's forgiveness. Giving Isaac pleasure and showing him what acceptance and desire could be like pleased me more than him sucking me off would anyway.

Better to give than to receive.

Fuck.

I scrubbed a hand over my face and strained my ears as Isaac went out the front door. Hurrying to the window overlooking the gravel parking area out front, I held my breath.

Hoping he wouldn't leave.

Unable to pray that he would.

He grabbed an overnight bag from the passenger seat, and my exhale rushed out.

Lips in a thin line, he stomped back toward the cottage.

The door slammed once more.

I eyed the wall, tracking his steps down the hallway, the squeak of the other bedroom hinges reassuring me he planned to do as I allowed.

Knowing I couldn't interact with him again that night without taking another of his firsts, I stayed put. Naked except for the towel. Listening as he settled in for the night.

Brushed his teeth.

Flushed the toilet.

But no bedroom door snicked or slammed shut.

He'd left it open on purpose, I didn't doubt. An invitation.

Shit.

I closed my eyes, my ears ringing in the stifling stillness.

A moan reached me.

Another.

Goddamnit. A muscle ticked in my jaw, but I quietly pulled my door open. His bedroom lay diagonal in the hallway, the angle too much for me to watch him jerk off.

I wanted—needed—to see him touch himself while thinking about me.

The craving to fill my eyes ghosted my feet forward, and I moved without introspection. Across the carpeted hallway. Hand on his opened door, I pushed it inward.

Isaac lay on his back, his hooded gaze on me while slowly jacking his length. Ten hot, slick-sounding seconds passed between us in silence before his lips parted. "I know you want me."

I couldn't deny the truth, couldn't stop watching the swollen head of his dick disappear beneath his palm and reappear between his fingers.

He rolled and lifted onto his knees, his ass on offer.

The pinkness of his rosebud made me salivate, and my dick twitched so damn hard it nudged the towel from my waist.

Sucking oxygen through my nose, I strode in, fisting myself. So much hunger for him rushed through my blood that I trembled.

It's not sin if I don't fuck him.

Clinging to that thought, I stood a foot away from his backside, his pale cheeks flexing as he continued to fuck his own hand.

He panted against the quilt.

Needy little brat. I should have swatted his ass

red for what he did to me, how he made me feel.

Instead, I fucked my hand hard and fast through a mess of precum, pulling and panting, urging my tingling balls to release.

Isaac whimpered, his hole clenching right in front of my eyes—and I fucking blew like a geyser, spurting up his back.

"Oh fuuuuck," he groaned, his hips jerking in time with mine while I painted his ass cheeks a milky white.

Even emptied, my dick throbbed to fill him. Stuff him full.

Claim and own him.

I backed away, my pulse thrumming, my breath coming in ragged gasps. My body shuddered from having ejaculated harder than I ever had in my life.

Towel, I reminded myself, glancing at where it lay on the floor.

I shut the door with a finality I didn't want to accept.

Closed myself in my own room, locking the door to keep the brat out even though I craved his presence in more than just my bed.

Collapsed on my mattress, my emotions completely spent.

Quiet thoughts.

And an hour later, I still lay in the dark, alone, wondering over the numbness coating my mind and my lack of guilt.

24

ISAAC

He left me.

On my knees, covered in his cum, my hand smeared with my own release.

Holy fucking hell.

A whispered giggle rushed from my lungs, and I slid my body forward, sprawling on the mess I'd made.

Shit, was that hot.

I giggled again as a shudder rippled through me. I'd never felt so damn sated. Emptied.

Malachi hadn't fucked my ass like I'd hoped he would, hadn't taken me up on that offer of my biggest first, but satisfaction, bone-deep and bright, flooded me.

I closed my eyes, uncaring of the stickiness beneath me, simply wanting to soak in the happiness until it tugged me into dreamless sleep.

Not cleaning up before passing out wasn't the smartest choice, and I regretted it the second I opened my eyes to an early sunrise.

I rolled, the quilt beneath my naked body sticking to my balls long enough to tug at my pubic hairs.

"Fuck." Grimacing, I peeled skin from material and flopped onto my back with an "oomph" escaping my smiling lips at the stretch of his cum dried across my skin.

I hated early mornings, but fuck, did I feel refreshed.

The thought of who laid across the hall pulled me off the bed, and I snagged a pair of shorts I'd put out the night before, tugging them on while trying not to stumble across the carpet.

He'd closed his bedroom door.

I eased the handle.

He'd locked the damn door.

Fucker.

Unable to rouse the energy to scowl, I moved toward the open area, eyeing the lake through the slider doors. Fog drifted above the water, dancing like teasing fingertips over the ripples.

My skin shivered for such a touch.

Grinning, I strode outside and filled my lungs with warm, clean air, scented with flowers and pine.

A gorgeous morning and sunrise.

A new beginning.

Happy fucking birthday to me.

My steps came faster as I strode across the small lawn. Even faster as my foot met the first board of the dock—and I sprinted the remainder of the way, diving at its end.

Cool water swept over my skin, welcoming me into its depths.

Smiling, I kicked and swept my arms back, bringing me to the surface in a gasped rush. Warm air once more kissed my face, and I treaded water, the cells in my body feeling refreshed.

This is what freedom feels like.

I laughed and dove back down, exerting excess energy like I'd done every summer since I could remember. Frolicking and attempting to push water from my path.

A good twenty minutes passed before I felt him.

Rising to the surface, I turned to find what I already knew.

Malachi stood on the porch with a coffee mug in hand. Shirtless, gym shorts hanging low on his hips.

Watching me.

Enough distance separated us that I couldn't tell if he frowned or smiled, but his body appeared relaxed. No tension rode his shoulders, no rigid stance. He simply drank his coffee.

Even more buoyancy lifted my spirits, and I swam toward shore with steady strokes, found my feet, and traipsed through leaf debris and sand until

I stepped onto dry land, water streaming down my limbs.

I hadn't thought to bring out a towel.

Malachi's gaze slid down over me, but my balls and dick were too damn chilled to so much as twitch.

I moved closer slowly, even though I wanted to sprint to him, afraid he might startle. "Morning," I greeted him from below the back deck, my head tipped to hold his gaze.

Sleepy blue eyes, sexy as fuck and vulnerable studied my face as he sipped from his mug. "Happy birthday."

My grin split open at his haggard morning voice. There was no stopping my emotions from spilling out. "Best one ever."

"Coffee?" he asked, motioning toward the cabin with his head.

"Sounds good." Other things sounded a hell of a lot better, but I would take him up on his offer since he hadn't come out scowling and telling me to get lost and move on with my life.

I sped up the deck's stairs, my feet barely landing on every other tread.

Malachi eyed my wet body for all of two seconds before turning away, his face unmoved. "Let me get you a towel."

I watched his ass as he walked back the hallway toward the bathroom, and I filled my eyes with every inch of his tanned, tattooed body as he approached again.

His shorts tented with a boner he hadn't sported while out on the deck, but he didn't bother using the towel in his hand to cover the evidence of what I did to him.

Malachi tossed the towel at my face, effectively tearing my focus off his dick.

Time to up my game.

25

———

MALACHI

I woke to the first rays of sunshine drifting over my face. As with every morning, I lay still, inhaling and shifting through consciousness. Most mornings, I forced my thoughts on prayer, starting the day right.

But I already felt right. Content. A quiet spirit.

Is this peace from You or because I didn't sin last night? Or is this because of him—Isaac being here—and me not wanting to be anywhere else?

Of course, He didn't answer.

Refusing to further question the serenity and happiness I'd been begging God to bless me with for months, I rolled from bed and tugged on some shorts.

Isaac's door stood open, his bed empty—quilt rumpled.

Had he slept? Left after I'd finally passed out?

My heart beat heavier in my chest, and I hurried toward the front of the house. A grunted exhale escaped me upon seeing his car still parked beside Dad's old truck. "Isaac?" I called, turning to look around the cottage.

He didn't reply.

A quick walk toward the sliders let me know where he'd gotten to.

His pale body cut through lake water like a knife, sure and steady, a haze of fog lingering mere feet above his head.

I realized I smiled while watching him enjoy his freedom. My contentment grew until I released a cleansing sigh. How could life suddenly feel so... damn perfect?

Having his body beneath mine would be even better.

Pushing down my morning wood that'd taken interest in Isaac, I ambled back into the kitchen area and pressed the Keurig's power button. After a quick visit to the bathroom to empty my bladder, my coffee sat ready and waiting. Steaming and fragrant enough to make me smile again.

The warmth of morning greeted me as I slid the door open and stepped out onto the back porch. That first sip of coffee poured down into my stomach, and I let out a silent groan of appreciation in my head.

Isaac still swam, and I enjoyed the sight of him while my taste buds thanked me over every swallow.

A murky lake cut by pale, toned arms—I imagined he smiled too.

Eventually, he treaded water, his head swiveling my way.

Did he see me grinning into my mug? Fighting off the outward expression of complete...happiness? Zero guilt rode my shoulders. No regret for my actions the night before. If anything, I regretted not taking the gift that he'd first offered.

And that truth didn't even manage to twinge my conscience. God, the Holy Spirit, sat quiet in my head, same as He'd always done, and for the first time, I didn't care.

I found peace in His silence.

Isaac swam toward shore, holding my stare and all my focus. He walked out of the water, dripping like a pale god of the lake, all lithe muscle and sinew I wanted to lick and bite from head to toe.

A beautiful creature—hardly unholy—one worthy of my affection, and my eyes drank him down as he neared.

"Morning," I managed to croak out, remembering being on my knees for him the night before. Pleasuring him.

Worshiping him.

His grin, the first real one I'd ever seen, stole my breath, and I didn't remember filling my lungs again until I passed from his sight to grab him a towel from the bathroom.

Giddiness lit my insides, and I didn't question my rising desire. I let it free in the tranquility I'd found, allowing my craving for him to swell inside me until my dick throbbed, tenting my shorts.

I tossed the towel in Isaac's face to take his focus off my groin, to hide his calculating gaze and sexy as fuck smirk.

I moved into the kitchen, listening as he dried himself off. "Milk and sugar?" I asked, placing another mug beneath the coffee maker.

"Sure."

"Do you even drink coffee?" I asked without glancing over my shoulder.

"I do now."

Still smiling like a dork, I made the eighteen-year-old's first cup of coffee, and I turned to find him a few feet away—exactly as my tingling skin had recognized. He accepted the mug, our fingers grazing which caused both our lengths to jerk.

Guess the cold lake's effects on him had faded.

I slid onto one of the kitchen chairs and watched him exhale over the mug's top, steam rising toward his nose.

He sipped.

"Well?"

A grimace twitched his lips. "Tastes like burnt water. How can you drink this shit?"

"It's fucking delicious." I slurped another hearty

sip myself and made an *Ahhh* noise after swallowing it down.

Isaac's focus stayed on my mouth, and I licked a droplet of coffee clear from my lower lip.

I didn't know what the hell had come over me, where the joy in my heart originated from, but I wasn't going to question it.

How *right* I felt inside.

My mind rested easy. God hadn't answered after years of begging, and I decided to let my emotions lead me since they had somehow found peace without a higher power.

"So, birthday boy," I said with a flirty tone, sitting back in my chair, my mug and hand propped on the table beside me. "What do you want?"

"You," he didn't hesitate to answer.

Isaac set his coffee on the counter, shoved his wet shorts to the floor, and straddled my lap as though I'd invited him to climb aboard. He snuggled in close, pressing his cool skin against my bare chest, soaking in the warmth I wanted to give.

Hell, I wanted him to take more from me. A shit ton, if my racing heart and throbbing dick were any indication.

"Hmm." I released my grip on my coffee mug that wasn't yet empty. I had better things to grasp. Like two plump ass cheeks, also cold to the touch. "You've got a great ass," I murmured, brushing my lips over his.

"It's yours whenever you're ready to claim it." He rocked against my straining length, sending a jolt through my entire body.

Fuck, he felt good on me.

"Hmm," I hummed again and licked along his tongue, waiting on guilt that never hit.

"You taste like coffee," he complained, angling his head away from my hungry mouth.

"You sat on my lap, brat. Deal with it or get off."

Those hazel eyes usually filled with disappointment and hurt smiled again as his lips curled upward. "I'd love to get off—after you give me my birthday present."

"And that would be...me." I didn't bother asking a question.

"Your dick." Isaac kissed my nose. "In my ass."

I pulled my head back to see his face better while sliding my fingers down between his cheeks, fingertips brushing over his hole.

His eyes rolled upward as I stroked with featherlight touches.

"Mmm, yes, please." A gulp sounded, his hazed over gaze capturing mine while he gyrated his hips, grinding against my dick.

My heart thrummed as I stared into his eyes, our souls connected in mutual need. "You're sure?"

"Let me have you," Isaac murmured, rocking again to rub our dicks together as I continued to play with his asshole. "And if your God wants to take me in return, it'll be worth the experience of having your body inside mine."

"It won't," I told him the truth, remnants of sorrow from losing Brian still buried in the deepest parts of my soul.

"It's my life." Isaac clasped my scruffy cheeks in his hands. "And if I want to be struck by lightning for fucking my youth pastor, that's my choice. Show me what it feels like to have a man own me, Malachi." He swallowed hard. "Love me."

Selfishness rose up inside me, an acute sense of determination. Giving Isaac what he craved could only bring me pleasure, and I wanted nothing more than to lavish that affection on him. Undivided attention. Because I could imagine what it would feel like—all the same things I'd always desired and had never found.

Warmth rushed through my body, centering in my groin, every inch of my skin tightening in readiness.

Sure, I damned us to eternal hell, but decision made, I stood, still grasping his ass. He wrapped his legs around my waist, holding tight. "My bed or yours?" I asked, heading toward the hallway with sure steps.

"I don't give a fuck," he stated, his voice husky. He was breathless. Eyes wide and shining. No hint of fear on his face.

I pushed in his bedroom door with my foot,

deciding I wasn't about to fuck him on his parents' bed.

Our gazes held, tethered tight, as I crawled onto the mattress before settling my body against his.

"You're so fucking beautiful," I murmured, smoothing his dark, damp hair off his forehead.

Of one mind, our mouths came together, both of us reaching for my shorts. A quick shimmy, lips still fused, and nothing separated us.

Skin on skin.

Heat and hard muscle from mouth to toes.

Two leaking dicks that rubbed with every thrust.

"Fuck, do you feel good," I groaned, holding his hair and relishing the precum slickened length of him sliding along mine.

"My ass will feel better."

I stilled and peered down at him. "I don't have any lube."

Goddamnit to fucking hell...

Isaac scrambled from beneath me, bending over to rifle through his bag.

That ass.

"Damn," I groaned, palming my dick to calm the fuck down.

He hopped back onto the bed, shoving his hand at me.

I glanced down. A packet of lube...and a condom. "Have you done this before?" I asked. The thought he'd been too prepared for a virgin, that someone had gotten to him before me, twisted my stomach up tight.

"No. Just hopeful." Still smiling, he tucked himself in front of me. On his back. Legs spread.

Smooth chest. Tight nipples. Rippling abs and gorgeous, prominent hip bones.

My focus dropped to his drawn-up balls, to the silky soft skin behind and the pink puckered hole beneath. Mouthwatering and beautiful to the point I grew feverish.

Isaac lay spread out like a goddamn buffet, and after having gone without for almost five years, I was ravenous. Setting aside the condom and lube, I leaned in to feast. I licked across his clavicle, tasting the lake and musk of him. All man. Fucking delicious.

He grasped my head as I closed my teeth over a nipple, his curse making my dick twitch against his restless thigh. Nibbling and biting, I made my way southward, exploring every inch of his tautness, nosing and licking. Shadow and light played over his body from the open window beside us as I familiarized myself with every inch of his torso.

Goosebumps rose along the damp trail my tongue left behind, his whimpers and moans like music to my damn ears.

The tip of his dick bumped my chin, and I moved to the side, scraping my scruff down his length.

"Oh fuck." He half sat, our gazes locked while I rubbed my face all over his dick, flicking out my tongue to taste the precum leaking from his tip. "Suck me, Malachi. Please fucking suck me."

"I've got a better idea." I grasped his thighs, spread him wide, and licked over his asshole.

"God," he groaned, falling back to the bed, head tipped, veins popping along his flushed neck. A shudder rippled over him as I licked again. "*Christ...* hell, yes."

My dick throbbed as I twirled my tongue around his hole, tasting and breathing in his musky scent.

He grabbed the back of his knees, spreading to give me better access, and I settled against the bed to eat him until he begged for more. The first probe of my tongue earned me a delicious gasp, and the second had him grabbing hold of his balls and whimpering.

"Feel good?" I asked and slid back in, loving how he tightly contracted around my tongue.

"Mmm." He choked on his moan and swallowed hard. The sight of him, eyes hazed with lust and lips parted to pant while watching me eat his ass, made my dick leak.

With a groan, I dove back in until his tight ring became soft beneath my attention.

"Do you like my tongue in your hole?" I asked, rubbing the pad of my thumb over him.

"Fuck yes." Rasped and thready, his needy voice

shot lust straight to my own balls. "M-more...please."

I pushed up to my knees, my saliva leaving his rosebud glistening and gorgeous.

I tore open the lube, not taking my eyes off where I craved to shove my dick. "You ever touch yourself down there?"

"Yeah." No hesitation, no embarrassment. Isaac knew who he was, what he wanted—and I'd never seen anything sexier.

Coating some fingers, I lifted my attention to his face. "Ready for me to stretch you?" I asked, teasing him in slow passes, gentle pressure on his pliant hole.

Pupils swelled, he moaned and pulled his knees back farther, opening himself up to me. "Yes. Fuck yes."

I slid one fingertip past his ring of muscle without resistance into tight heat.

"Fuuuck," he groaned, the tendons in his neck sticking out.

Teeth clenched over the thought of his body sucking my dick in like that, I pressed in little more.

He hissed, his eyes closing, but no discomfort lined his forehead.

A few more tender, shallow strokes, and I rotated my hand while sliding in deep to rub over his prostrate.

"Jesus! Fuck." He arched his back, head pressing

hard against the mattress before he grabbed hold of his balls and tugged.

"Mmm." I couldn't help but moan my agreement. It'd been five years since I'd been with a man, but I hadn't lost my touch, thank fuck.

Sliding in a second finger brought on a slight grimace to his face, but he held my gaze, his pouty lips parting again, the pulse in his neck throbbing.

"Okay?" I asked, my voice as strangled as my fingers inside his ass.

"Oh yeah," he whispered, lifting his hips in offering for me to take more.

Sweat beaded on his brow as I worked him open, alternating scissoring to stretch him and rubbing his prostrate. His whimpers and moans made my balls pulse, and I added to the wet sounds of finger fucking by palming myself to smear precum down my length.

"Please, Malachi." He shifted, bobbing his leaking dick over his abs. "I-I'm ready."

Yes.

I pulled my fingers from him, and they shook while sheathing up my dick. A little more lube down over my length and I leaned forward, holding my base.

A pause caught my breath as our gazes locked.

The perfect time for guilt to rise, for my conscience to whisper about the sin I planned to commit.

Nothing rose to mind. No booming voice from the heavens promising fire and brimstone. Not a goddamn thing other than wanting to give pleasure to the young man I felt tethered to the deepest reaches of me.

I released a slow exhale, the responsible part of me needing to give him one last out. "This is what you want?" I placed the head of my dick against his hole and pressed forward enough he'd pay attention to the start of a stretch beyond mere fingers. "To be sodomized? Used for some pervert's pleasure?"

He held my stare, eyes hazed with passion. "I want to be used for *your* pleasure."

No man had ever offered me what Isaac did. Others had taken, gladly received—but they'd never freely given of themselves to me—*for* me.

Heat swelled inside my chest, an ache I'd never felt before—and I needed to share whatever it was with Isaac. I needed to be one with him, deeply imbedded in his soul.

I pushed, breaching his body, and he gasped, teeth clenched over owning the head of my dick.

Insane compression...strangling, perfect heat.

"Fuck are you tight," I groaned through clenched teeth. Glancing down, I watched my dick sink in another inch. Pulling out to the head again made Isaac hiss, but I pushed right back in, gaining ground and damn near swooning over how his ass sucked at my girth, welcoming and wanting. "Goddamn..." I repeated the action, my focus on his face. His furrowed brow. The lower lip caught between his teeth.

I should have felt concern over his obvious discomfort, but I found myself smirking from the bubbling happiness inside me. My quads tensed with the desire to stab into his body, to claim and own.

"Relax, brat," I murmured, grasping his thighs and spreading him wider. "Take the dick you've been begging for."

One last thrust bottomed me out in exquisite heat.

"Oh shit. Oh shit." He lifted his head and grabbed hold of my forearms, panting, his gaze glued to where I'd buried myself in his hot body.

"Holy fuck, Isaac." I fought to keep my focus on his flushed face rather than letting my eyelids fall shut at the perfect sensation of being inside him.

"Fucking hell." Isaac laid back, neck straining, eyes closed as his hole clenched around me. "Fucking *hell,* give me a second. Fuck, fuck, fuck..."

I wanted to devour him, to destroy his ass with years of pent-up lust, but more than that, I wanted him to savor the satisfaction of his birthday gift—needed it—and he had to be present for me to enjoy it. I leaned over him, cradling his face even though he still held tight to my arms. "Hey."

His long lashes fluttered as he opened his eyes.

Like a punch to my gut, a rush of longing, a craving for more than just the physical with Isaac filled me up, making my chest ache.

"Relax, baby. Just look at me—stay with me, okay?" My voice broke.

Baby...I hadn't used any term of endearment since Brian—but calling Isaac that seemed right. Perfect in a way no other name had before.

Isaac's lower lip slid back between his teeth, but he nodded. Moving one hand behind my head, he gripped tight like his ass did around my dick.

"I'll make it good for you, I promise. Just stay with me." I swiped my mouth over his, covering him with my body and kissing him until he went liquid. Lips soft. Hands grasping at my back, my hair. Heels digging into my ass, keeping *me* in the present.

Go time.

26

———

ISAAC

Malachi dizzied me with his mouth, distracting me from the thick dick shoved up my ass until I could relax at the invasion. He backed out, dragging his length from my body. One slow, steady push buried him balls deep, and I moaned against his lips, the initial stretch and sting of penetration dissolving into absolute, ridiculous pleasure of being stuffed full.

Two more gentle pull and push movements and I clutched at him, no longer relaxed. Energy raced over my skin, buzzing my cells with enough current to light a bulb. I'd played with my ass before while jerking off, but fingers didn't compare to the girth of Malachi's dick.

He finally filled me up, became one with me beyond connected gazes and mutual longing.

"Oh God, Malachi—so fucking good." I bit at his

lips, whimpering. Going out of my fucking mind over being stuffed full of *him*. "So, so good." I continued to chant in my head, lifting my hips to meet his every stroke.

Experiencing the dream of Malachi's dick, every slick glide of him into me—inside my damn head and heart—*that* was fucking heaven. Damn perfection.

He planked and gave me more, thrusting rather than rocking in and out. He held my gaze, his blue eyes hazed with passion, and I clutched at his biceps, my heels tugging him in closer.

So much closer.

I wanted our souls entwined, fucking like our bodies did.

Precum leaked from my bobbing dick, oozing onto my abs that contracted with every push from Malachi. My balls ached, seized up and ready to explode, but I wasn't ready. Needed it to last longer. For an eternity.

His lower lip looked plumper, parted from the thinner upper one. I wanted to bite it. Lick it. Suck it.

"Give me your mouth," I begged, barely recognizing my own voice as ragged as it was.

He shifted his knees for a different angle and drove in while lowering his weight again, rubbing my prostate and trapping my dick between our bodies.

Fucking fireworks exploded behind my eyelids at

the delicious friction on my length, and I groaned against his lips.

"Gonna come, baby?" he whispered over my mouth, the nickname bursting bubbles of pure joy inside my belly.

"Yeah." I gasped and clamped down on his lower lip with my teeth, holding on while he slid his abs oh so fucking perfectly over my dripping length.

Oh yeah.

My balls let loose, and wet heat spurted between our bodies, creating a slick mess for him to slide through while stabbing into my spasming ass.

His grunts and groans rushed my blood and made my ears ring.

Heaven buzzed me higher than any joint, and I floated in an ocean of euphoria without a care in the world as Malachi fucked into me over and over, pushing my back along the bed in his attempts to bury deeper.

"Isaac," he whispered my name with a gasp—and shuddered, his dick jerking inside my ass. His deep groan while coming sent a shiver through me that twitched my flagging dick.

I clung to him and licked at his lips as he panted, his head hanging above mine. One last tremor made him go limp in my arms, and he kissed me, his full weight heavy against my chest.

Our hearts raced together, skin and bone separating their life-giving thumps as reality returned.

Slow, languid kisses between us continued long after he pulled out of my sore backside and got rid of the condom. His caressing hands offered affection, giving what I craved until we lay spent. Sweaty and sated. A sticky, perfect mess.

No fucking way were we wrong.

The connection between us only intensified from what I had begged for. I'd never felt so cherished. Accepted.

Whole.

Malachi was all I'd imagined. He was all I could ever want.

"Worth being struck down for?" he asked without a hint of teasing, his eyes unreadable when he finally lifted his head from the crook of my neck where he'd rested for a full on five minutes of peaceful silence.

"Fuck yes—but no one is going to smote me for my supposed sins," I told him, rubbing my hand over his jaw so he would lean into the touch like he'd done a half-dozen times since gifting me the best birthday present ever. "That's your issue. Not mine."

Malachi kissed my palm, the act showing more intimate emotion than the kiss he brushed over my lips a second later.

"I loved how you said my name while coming," I told him, the memory burned into my head for life. Spank bank material and then some.

Our gazes locked, and the contentment, the

complete lack of guilt in his eyes resonated with me. "I couldn't think about anything but you in that moment. Couldn't...I just..."

Smiling, I held him tight as he shoved his face back into my neck and breathed deep, his expanded lungs pressing me firmly into the bed. "Yeah," I whispered, closing my eyes, my heart lighter than it'd ever been. "Me too."

———

The openness between us lingered as we showered together, Malachi offering me full access to his body with his soap. I sudsed him from neck to toes, running my hands over swells and dips, my favorite being the V between his hips.

I jacked his stiffening dick a few times but continued on with my job, loving the coarseness of his leg hair against my palms. I learned his ticklish spots—behind his knees and his ankles of all places —and I learned the areas to touch if I wanted to make him moan. Perineum and balls.

My tongue on both, I sucked at clean skin and the water cascading over his chest and onto my face.

For the first time in my life, I licked up the back of a dick to the salty pre-cum smearing at his slit. Malachi's. My own length leaked at that reality.

"God." He moaned and took hold of my face, allowing me to go at my own pace—learning his flavor, the shape of his swelling head, the silken feel of him over my tongue. "Yes," he hissed, his fingers tightening in my hair. "Just like that."

I moved my mouth over him, holding the weight of his balls in my hands. Kneading. Tugging when they drew up.

"Isaac..."

I took him deep until I gagged, earning me another dick-twitching groan.

"Do you know how many times I fantasized about you choking on my dick?" he rasped, shooting lust straight to my groin.

Fuck.

My dick jerked between my thighs, and I grabbed hold of my balls to keep from shooting off before he came.

He fucked my face a few more thrusts, gagging me each time before pulling me up and into his arms.

He ate at my mouth without restraint, no hesitation or apology for his hunger. And the heat in his eyes when he pulled back showed no reservations. "I want you."

"I'm yours," I told him, breathless as hell.

We both stilled. Staring. Lost in lust—but more than just the need to fuck, for me, at least. I meant what I'd said—this was beyond the physical. It always had been.

Emotion in his eyes rolled over me and filled me

the fuck up, leaving no room for depression, doubt, or desire for anything, anyone but him.

If he asked me to not leave, to put aside my dreams for Nashville, I would gladly agree.

Instead, he pulled me from the shower, dragged me into the bedroom without either of us drying off, and shoved me back onto the bed.

I sprawled happily, even though I wasn't so sure my asshole would be that thrilled with what the heat in his eyes promised. Regardless, I wasn't about to say no. Never in a million fucking years.

"Lube?" he asked, grabbing my bag off the floor.

"Side pocket." I laced my fingers behind my head even though my heart thrummed in anticipation. My hole clenched, but I continued to feign confidence over the thought of taking him inside my body again.

My dick was on board. Hard and leaking.

He climbed onto the bed, yanked my legs out straight, and straddled me.

My hands found his thighs.

"I want you," he repeated and tore open the condom.

"Show me how much," I said rather than stating he already had me whenever, however—

He rolled the condom down over my dick.

"Oh shit." I gulped, contracting my abs to raise my head and watch him smear lube down over my length, slowly jacking me, slickening every inch. He was going to put my dick inside his ass. Allow me to own him. "Fucking hell, Malachi."

"Can I?"

"Are you fucking kidding me right now?" I asked, my voice shaking from the adrenaline rushing through my blood.

My fingers clenched his thighs as he lifted and positioned my throbbing dick against his hole. He hadn't prepped.

Our eyes clashed.

"Malachi, shouldn't you—"

He sank down onto me, ripping whatever I'd planned to say from my lungs.

Malachi's body sucked me in without resistance until his ass rested against my groin. Tighter than any fist. Hotter than any hand or mouth. Pure, wicked torture, an overload of sensation...

"Jesus." I gasped, a full-on body tremor moving me beneath him from the absolute *fucking* perfection of being inside his body. "Jesus...fuck."

He planked, his blue eyes holding me captive, his asshole clenching around my girth. "So fucking wrong," he whispered, shifting forward and fucking himself back onto my dick.

"So fucking *right*," I tossed back, grabbing hold of his flexing thighs as he repeated the motion.

I trembled beneath him, the need to move, to fuck like an animal—barely restrained passion—

keeping me rigid. Teeth clenched, I watched his face, his slack mouth as he used my body.

"Malachi," I whispered through clenched teeth, my short fingernails digging into his thighs.

"Fuck me."

Christ...

I thrusted to meet him, my breath leaving in a rush over how deeply I buried into his tight hole.

He groaned, head tipping upward, spine arching. "Fuck, you feel good, Isaac. So thick and hard."

My balls seized up against my body at his haggard tone.

"Wish you were bare," he said, as we slid apart and slammed back together again. "Want to feel your cum inside me."

Holy fucking shit.

"Don't talk dirty to me, or I'm gonna blow like the untried brat I am," I stated through clenched teeth, trying to stave off my building orgasm.

"Mmm." He smirked down at me, moving over me like a sex god. The look on his face was so far removed from the stoic Malachi I'd already fallen for that my heart ached along with my balls. "Don't blow yet, baby. Let me ride you."

Baby...

"Fucking hell," I muttered, tearing my focus from his lust-filled eyes to check out where his hot ass swallowed my dick.

Back and forth, slick glides, and clamping heat.

So damn good—I needed to tug down on my balls but couldn't reach them.

Don't blow like a damn kid. Don't blow. Don't blow...

Couldn't see. Goddamnit, I wanted to *see* my dick owning his ass.

"Want to take over?"

"Hell yeah." I shoved at Malachi, desperate to get between his thighs like I'd had wet dreams about, never in a million years thinking I'd experience that side of heaven.

He rolled and raised his legs, hands clasping the backs of his knees. Thick, dripping cock. Blond curls around his tight balls. Lube-slickened hole that looked way too small to take my girth even though it had stretched for me seconds earlier.

My limbs shook as I crowded in close, a little unsure of myself even while my length throbbed to sink deep again.

"Put your dick inside me."

"Holy fuck." I gulped and pressed the tip of my length against his puckered hole.

"Give it to me, Isaac."

Fuck, when he said my name like that...

I squeezed my base and inhaled a shuddering breath to get ahold of myself. One slow push forward and his ass sucked me in like a greedy bitch —all the way in, balls deep. Curses spilled from my clenched teeth as I held still, fighting to not ejaculate at the clear sight of my dick—*mine*—buried inside Malachi Foley's body.

"Fuck. I... Shit." I gulped again, my fingers digging into his thighs.

"Move."

I blinked and found Malachi watching me, brow furrowed, lower lip tempting me to bite.

Backing out damn near made my eyes roll into my head, but I moved forward and grasped his lip between my teeth. He grunted into my mouth with every thrust as my body took over. Fucking without thought. Harder. Deeper—not damn near deep enough.

He didn't complain about my erratic, frantic movements but locked his heels around my ass and pulled me into him forcibly and fast, his hips rising to meet mine.

And it was me who whisper-hollered his name while coming, me who ended up smearing his cum all over our torsos when rubbing my body into his while breathing against his neck.

Absolute. Fucking. Heaven.

27

MALACHI

We walked through my pastor's cottage in nothing but shorts slung low on our hips. Shoulders brushing, hands groping more than once while gathering supplies to make a late breakfast.

I kissed the back of his neck as he poured batter onto the griddle, and he ground his ass against my groin. The scent of sausage frying on the stovetop filled my nose, making my stomach growl, but I felt more ravenous for the young man in my arms than food.

Holding onto his chest, his back hot and solid against mine, I slid my hand down over his torso, fingertips mapping out every indent between muscle and bone.

"You're perfect," I murmured against his ear, knowing he couldn't be told that fact often enough.

Isaac set aside the batter and turned, grabbing my hips to bring our groins together. Both spent but still wanting.

I kissed him, licking at the fresh cinnamon flavor of his mouth, groaning at how the emptiness in my chest had completely dissipated. He felt good beneath my hands and even better in my heart.

Pulling back, I studied his face. Lips pink and swollen from kissing. Cheeks flushed, eyes free from shadows and...happy.

"I'm not sorry," I told him quietly, smoothing his hair back from his face.

He clutched at my hips, keeping me close. "I was afraid you would be."

So open...when he'd been closed off, cryptic, and hurting before.

"I don't know what it is," I went on, needing to make him understand what I wasn't even sure I did. "I—I've been begging God to fill me, to give me peace and joy, but He never has. All through Bible college, I felt empty, going through the motions in the hope I did right."

He smirked as though he knew where I headed.

"Brat."

Isaac's smile widened, but I kissed it away.

"Pancakes," he whispered against my mouth, and I let him go so he could turn and tend to our breakfast.

I wrapped my arms around his waist and settled my chin on his shoulder while he flipped the golden discs over. "My chest isn't hollow anymore."

"Neither is mine."

A shuddering sigh rippled through me. "I'm happy for the first time in I don't know how long."

"Same."

"They say you can't find joy in others unless you're content with yourself."

Isaac turned again, rubbing his palm along my scruffy jaw. I leaned into his touch, closing my eyes.

"I'm calling bullshit on that one," he stated with absolute assurance.

Chuckling, I kissed his palm. "Why's that?"

"Because you make me feel normal. Accepted. *That* makes me happier than I've ever been—no fucking way is it wrong."

I couldn't argue with his logic. Didn't want to. So I kissed him again before releasing my hold on his luscious body.

"Breakfast." One last peck to his lips and I tore myself away.

Five pancakes and four sausages later, I sat nursing another cup of coffee while he finished eating.

"Do your parents know where you are?"

"No. They probably think I'm halfway to Nashville by now."

The idea of him leaving for Tennessee at the end of...whatever it was we were doing made my stomach churn, and I shifted on my chair.

He glanced up, his gaze questioning. "What's wrong?"

I smiled to ease his obvious tension, hoping to do the same for me. "Nothing. Want to take out the canoe?"

Isaac studied my face for a few seconds, but just when I felt sure he was going to call me out for lying, he nodded. "Sure."

———

We spent the afternoon on the lake, swimming when it got too hot, only heading out in the canoe for a half hour before agreeing the seats were too damn hard on our sore asses.

Refreshing laughter infused every conversation, even when he asked about Brian, and I shared it all. Everything he wanted to know. How I'd talked the shy, gay kid into sneaking around with me, even at church, taking advantage of darkened corners and closets for hand and blow jobs.

For the first time, my heart didn't ache at the memories, and I wondered over the reason. The pink skin of the young man who'd been out in the sun too long, the full, smiling lips, the hazel eyes glancing down over my body every so often...Isaac was so much more to me than Brian ever had been.

He understood why I'd struggled to make the "right" choices and the high expectations placed on me by my God-fearing parents, even though mine had been loving in their leading. We shared the loneliness we'd endured due to the secret parts of us and the craving of affection, of unconditional love from another man.

The need to be ourselves outside of what we'd been force-fed and what I'd dragged my ass back into due to a promise made to my gracious mom.

Or perhaps I'd lived and learned enough to move on from past wounds.

Either way, I gloried in the freedom from sorrow and simply enjoyed the stories I shared with him.

Isaac had no such past to admit to other than fingering himself and jerking off to porn while imagining the only guy he'd craved.

Me. His youth pastor, a man forbidden to him but too tempting to ignore.

"I wanted you to follow me to our bunk room that night up in Maine."

His smirk was contagious, and I filled my eyes with him rather than the small fire we'd built together for s'mores after our grilled chicken dinner. "I knew you were going to be trouble from the start."

"*Just a man,*" Isaac repeated what I'd told him all

those months ago. He snorted and laced his fingers through mine resting on my thigh. "You're ten times more than most."

"You haven't met that many men," I said, my lips losing their upward tilt.

"Don't get all insecure on my ass."

I raised an eyebrow his way, but he left his lawn chair for my lap, the one beneath me creaking as he settled sideways across my thighs. "This thing might not hold us both."

"Don't give a shit. I've got something to tell you, and I don't want you to see anything but me when I say it."

I gave Isaac my full attention, our arms naturally finding their way around the other.

"I'm young."

Too damn young.

"And my life is only beginning." He studied my face, but I didn't hide. I wanted honesty. Needed it after a lifetime of lies. "But I know who my heart and body craves. This isn't just a bunch of firsts for me like marks on some board of accomplishments, Malachi. I want this. Us. And if that means no Nashville for me, then I'll gladly give it up."

For once, I hadn't needed to pull teeth. Isaac opening up, utter honesty from those lips...I'd never seen or heard such a beautiful thing. But being a selfish bastard at my core, I lusted for more. A tightening of that connection between us, that part inside him that called to me.

"Do you have your guitar with you?" I rasped, my heart near to bursting.

"Yeah."

I brushed my thumb over his lower lip. "Will you sing for me?"

Isaac hopped up without a word and disappeared around the side of the cottage.

The fire popped as I soaked in the meaning of his words—and the ones he'd written and put to song.

Was it possible for an eighteen-year-old kid to know his heart and mind? Was it possible our stolen moments together…could last? A new ache, a sweet one, swept through my chest, and I rubbed at my T-shirt, wondering at the strangeness of it. Not hurt but not joy.

Pleasure/pain, an addictive feeling.

The sun slowly sank beyond the opposite shore of the lake, sending a rainbow of color through the sky overhead. An end to my final day of vacation…

I had no idea what our future held. The thought I wouldn't have a job much longer, that I'd let down my mom settled on my shoulders, weighing me down and stealing some of my happiness—but not entirely. Nothing would stop the ebb of rightness I'd found in my soul.

And another thing I knew for certain—I wasn't about to let Isaac set his dreams aside.

Whistling, he rounded the cottage with his guitar case in hand, and I let out a sigh, my lips tilting upward again.

He settled into his chair and fiddled with the strings until his strumming fingers sounded right in both our ears. With a soft smile on his lips, he started plucking out the tune I recognized from Maine.

He sang to me like he'd done that night when I'd been swamped down by guilt, sharing his heart, his thoughts through music.

Broken.

Bleeding.

His tone rolled over me, his gaze held mine, and the desire sweeping over us stirred my entire body to life, pushing my worries aside for another day.

Wanting to fall. Worship you.

Needing you.

Without words to beg for your touch.

I sat struck dumb, same as the first time, unable to tear my stare off his beautiful face. His fingers manipulated the guitar's strings, gifting my ears with a haunting melody...

Energy buzzed through my veins, my entire body tingling with the urge to take him into my arms again, breathe him in, taste his kiss. Those sexy as fuck lips formed words that struck my heart with understanding.

Love.

The notes faded into the darkness growing around us.

"You wrote that about me."

The duck of his head, the shy smirk affirmed my statement.

"Sing it again."

He did—and the second he reached the chorus I'd caught the melody of, I joined in harmony. Isaac's voice cracked at the first couple of notes of us sensually rising, entwining, but he focused on my mouth like I did his, his tone growing sturdy once more with every word we sang together.

Beautifully.

Over and under, I weaved notes through his, and my pulse thrummed from the thrill, the absolute joy of creating magic with the young man who'd managed to weasel his way into my head and heart.

And later that night as he slept beside me, cramped on his tiny twin bed, I evaluated the fullness inside me. The contentment.

All I'd been searching for in the church, in the Bible...love, excitement, passion—life—I'd found with him. I settled my head onto the pillow we shared, tugging him just a bit closer, even though our skin touched from chest to toes.

What I felt for Isaac went far beyond my relationship with Brian, the one I'd thought had been my love, my partner for life. I'd survived his death, but I knew I wouldn't survive Isaac's.

I couldn't live without him.

I wouldn't.

But as always, I couldn't find the words to beg a God I'd begun to question to let me keep him.

28

ISAAC

I normally hated Sunday mornings with a passion, but opening my eyes and becoming conscious of why I was hot and sweaty brought a rush of adrenaline, an excitement to start the day.

Malachi.

In my bed, our limbs tangled.

Shifting my head on the pillow we shared, I found his lips slack, parted in sleep.

Hair getting too long on top and curling. Blond scruff lining his jaw and cheeks. Pale lashes lying still beneath his eyes. His slightly crooked nose and freckles darkened from our hours in the sun the day before.

So gorgeous.

I wanted to bite him, lick him awake, but I settled for relaxing there while facing him and just soaking the sight in. Enjoying the chance to study his face.

Etching it into my memory forever so one day I could die a happy man.

A humid summer breeze drifted across my skin from the open window behind me, doing little to cool me off as the sweat between our torsos worsened.

The thought of cool water promised relief and twitched my legs with the need to move. I couldn't lay still. And Malachi looked dead to the world. His non-morning ass would need coffee to wake up, and my body already buzzed with readiness for the day.

His heavy breathing didn't hitch as I slid from beneath his arm. Grinning, I took one last, long look over his sprawled body as he settled onto his belly... muscular back, rounded ass. Powerful thighs I'd scratched the hell out of while he'd fucked my sore ass before I passed out the night before.

I tested my backside with a little clench of my ass cheeks, grimacing over the ache left behind from his plundering.

But my dick swelled at the thought of doing it again.

Shaking my head, I forced my feet to carry me away, grabbed my shorts, and headed outside.

No haze of fog hung over the lake, just pure sunshine's rays as it peeked over the trees behind me.

We'd slept in—not surprising, considering how long we'd stayed up "sinning."

Best damn night of my life.

Freedom tasted better than I'd imagined too.

I dove into the water, mentally muttering an *Ah* as the coolness slid over my skin, washing away the sweat and remnants of cum from my belly. My throat decided in that moment to let me know how parched it felt, that I'd never dragged my ass from bed the night before to slake the thirst from fucking for an eternity.

Kicking and gyrating like a mermaid brought me back up to the surface, and I swiped the water from my eyes, checking on the front of the house.

No Malachi yet.

Taking my ass must have worn the old man out.

Snorting a chuckle, I backstroked a few yards, staring up into the sky emptied of clouds. Two birds flitted overhead, one chasing the other.

I thought again of heading to shore for some much-needed water, but I closed my eyes and told myself I'd go back soon. Too many delicious, tumbling thoughts filled my head, demanding my attention.

I'd meant what I'd said about giving up Nashville for him. If he asked me to stay by his side wherever he ended up, I would—because his job as my dad's youth pastor sure as fuck would end the second we returned to Elkins.

Imagining Dad's reaction to seeing us together, hands held, filled me with renewed giddiness as I cut through the water again. Warmth infused my muscles with every steady stroke leading me farther from shore.

A slight cramp grabbed hold of my calf, and I rolled to my back again, hoping to breathe the relentless ache away.

Blue sky. Yellow sun. Cheerful, chirping birds.

Never had I enjoyed a morning more, never had I felt such contentment.

All because of Malachi. His touch, his kisses, his acceptance.

I'd found heaven on earth, and nothing and no one would take it from me.

29

MALACHI

The scent of Isaac's skin and cum filled my nose, and I buried my face in the pillow, sniffing as wakefulness came over me. I reached for him, needing to know the night before hadn't been a dream.

I lay alone in his bed.

Lifting my head, I blinked with bleary eyes at the sunlight in the window.

The hell time is it?

I sat and rubbed a hand over my face, my stubble starting to itch.

Gotta shave.

But first...

"Isaac?" He didn't answer to my call, and I didn't hear him moving around the cottage. After a quick stop in the bathroom to empty my aching bladder, I shuffled into the kitchen.

No dreamy, pink-sunned skin and pouty lips.

Coffee.

Scratching at the dried remnants of cum around my groin, I flicked on the Keurig.

Awareness tickled along my nape—but not the energy that let me know Isaac entered the room. I turned, my gaze going to the slider and lake beyond. A sense of...something...urged me to go, and my feet moved on instinct.

I slid the door open. "Isaac?" I called, quickly glancing around the back yard, fire pit, and dock. "Isaac?"

"Mal—!"

I whipped toward the edge of the cove, my heart hitching at the cut off holler. A dark head bobbed in the lake along the edge of where placid waters met the current. He sank. Reappeared.

"Isaac!" I screamed and sprinted across the yard, an overwhelming sense of dread choking off my oxygen.

An arm flailed.

The water stilled.

No, no, no! Don't You dare do this to me again!

I dove into the water, still screaming at God in my head, strong strokes taking me toward where I'd seen Isaac last. Adrenaline coursed through me, giving me speed I wouldn't usually have, and I pulled up to the spot, treading water, spinning in circles.

"Isaac!" I shrieked, nausea rolling in my stomach. Nothing.

I dove, but the murky water proved too hard to see through within a matter of feet beneath the surface.

There was no God in that moment. No guiding light, no silent Holy Spirit prompting me in the right direction.

Just anguish and anger—and the deepest regret that I might not be able to experience a full life with Isaac.

You're no God of love.

I went back under, pain etched in the back of my throat.

Resurfaced and went down again, the sensation of things moving too slowly rippling over me.

Coming up empty, my chest hollowed out with every agonizing second that passed.

I've done everything to please you. Denied myself for years. And for what? Fuck you, and fuck the supposed truth of that book men claimed you wrote.

Isaac had been right. Even if God existed, I'd rather burn in hell than worship the kind of narcissistic tendencies he portrayed.

"Isaac!" I choked out a sob as my legs and arms grew weary, yet still I spun in a circle, searching the water around me and the dark trees on shore, the sun glinting and blinding me.

Isaac... Fuck.

I sobbed, blinking in the bright sunlight, turning my face from its golden rays, and allowing the current to take me southward—toward shore —toward...

A body bobbed feet away from the edge of a neighboring cottage.

Fresh adrenaline burst through me, and I cut across the water with precise movements, no longer tired.

He's okay...he's going to be okay.

Because if he wasn't, I couldn't go on.

30

ISAAC

Malachi screamed my name, but I couldn't draw breath to reply. I managed the first syllable before water closed over my head, filling my mouth. Choking me.

Should have gone back...

My calf continued to cramp from dehydration, the agony making it impossible to kick, and my arms had long since failed me.

Malachi.

I kicked with all I had left in my good leg, but exhaustion burned through my muscles.

Water crested over my face.

Sunlight.

I lifted a hand toward the warmth, but I sank again.

So tired.

Darkness crowded in, and there was no God. No emotion.

Just silence.

I floated, blinking, no longer choking.

Waiting for blinding light. The pearly gates. Or fire and brimstone.

But there was nothing, just the darkness creeping in, closing over me and offering peaceful, quiet freedom—

Fuck, how my lungs burned.

Hell is real after all.

"Fucking breathe!"

I coughed—and liquid rushed from my stomach. My lungs expanded.

Agony knifed my chest.

I vomited again, heaving and gagging.

"Isaac." Strong hands lifted me the second I sagged. Held me as I fought to inhale through the feeling of jagged glass that cut through my lungs. "Damnit, Isaac." Malachi sobbed, clutching me against him.

It took me a few seconds of shivering to realize we sat on shore.

I blinked at blinding sunlight, pulling blessed oxygen into my aching lungs and becoming conscious enough to take stock of my body. Cold. So cold. Teeth-clattering and body aching.

"You're not dead. Thank fuck you're not dead."

Malachi kept muttering. He looked me full in the face, his brow furrowing as he finally came into vivid focus. He smoothed my hair back as water dripped off his and onto my face. "You're okay," he murmured, kissing my forehead. "You're okay. Okay."

We rocked back and forth, and I burrowed against his warm muscle, listening to the steady thump of his heart.

Not dead—but I'd been there.

"Your b-beliefs are sh-shit," I rasped out and coughed, closing my eyes and remembering the darkness as his lips pressed to my forehead. "There's no b-bright light. No p-pearly gates. Only darkness. Accidents."

A tremor wracked through me in Malachi's arms, and he clutched me closer, his arms a vise. "I know."

My first free inhale left in a rush, and I smiled against the softness of his skin I never thought I'd feel again. He'd saved me. The one I worshiped—my Malachi.

31

MALACHI

Isaac didn't want to go to the hospital, but I wouldn't bend. The twist in my stomach wouldn't rest until I had him checked out even though he swore it'd been nothing but a damn leg cramp due to dehydration that had gotten the best of him.

We weren't in the ER for more than an hour hooked up to an IV for fluids before being given the green light he'd be just fine. I inhaled an unrestricted breath for the first time since seeing him go under the water.

We got back to the cottage, and I took him into the shower with me, holding him close and soaking in the warmth of his skin, the steady pulse of the blood pumping throughout his body.

Alive. Breathing.

The peace, the joy I'd been searching for, had

landed in my arms unexpectedly. Contentment and happiness hadn't come from submitting to God's will or from following a dark path he'd refused to light for me.

No. I'd found what my soul longed for in a young man. One who understood my struggles, my mind's workings even when I'd pushed him away in my attempts to stay "pure." He'd given my soul light when I needed it. Flooded my heart with emotion I'd craved for years. I wouldn't ever put distance between us again in any way. Nothing would take him from me—no one.

"Refusing you was slowly killing me," I murmured against his hair, holding his head to my chest. "I had no hope for a fulfilled life because I was missing a piece of myself. *Denying* an important part of myself."

A shudder ripped through me at memories of the emptiness I'd wasted time waiting for faith to fill.

Isaac's arms squeezed around me tighter, keeping us close, without a hint of air between our bodies as warm water cascaded down over us.

"And when you almost drowned today..." I swallowed hard, the truth sending a shudder through my body. "I realized I'd almost lost my heart, the peaceful place I'd been searching for."

Begging God and striving toward, I added in my mind. An empty, useless endeavor that had only gifted me with guilt and heavy heartedness.

But no more. I'd found my truth, the path I would gladly traverse through life.

With Isaac—my light. My salvation.

He looked me full on in the face, his eyes full of emotion I could feel swirling in my chest, tethering us together.

"I survived the sorrow of Brian's death, but I wouldn't survive losing you," I told him, tears welling for at least the tenth time since I'd dragged him from the water and performed CPR. Beat his chest. Demanded he breathe for me. Stay with me.

Isaac laid his head against me again, melting in my arms. His fingertips trailed down my back, offering tender affection. "You saved me," he whispered, his lips ghosting over my skin.

"I'd wanted to save you from *yourself* for the past couple of months," I reminded him, and he pulled back to peer at me, his gaze soft and vulnerable, "but you're perfectly you, Isaac. *Everything* about you is perfect. Don't ever change. Be you. Chase your dreams and be free."

"So you're saying you want me to take off without you."

"Fuck no." I yanked him back against me, the thought of him leaving me behind bring bile up the back of my throat. "I'm just saying that if loving you is a sin, is wrong, then I don't want to be right."

"So cliche."

"Shut up, brat."

He chuckled and bit my nipple.

"Ow!" I jerked away, backing into the hot spray.

"You really ought to get these pierced," he said, squeezing my hard nub, his lips quirking up in a teasing grin.

The time for reflection had come to an end. "Yeah?"

"That'd be sexy as fuck." He climbed up my body and wrapped himself around me, his hazel eyes filling with a look I recognized, one that made me hard within seconds. "The doctor said to take it easy," I told him.

"And the book you believe in—"

"Past tense," I growled.

"—says we'll burn in hell, but I don't give a shit. I want to feel you moving inside me bare with nothing between us, reminding me I'm alive. That we didn't lose what we've just found." His voice broke at the end, betraying a vulnerability I wanted to protect for eternity.

He wound his fingers around my neck, pressing in close, and my hard dick poked at his ass as he ground against me. "Loving you in this lifetime would be worth burning for eternity," I whispered, my focus on his pouty lower lip.

"Love, huh?" His lips curled up, and I leaned in to lick across the seam, water from the shower coating my tongue.

"*Love.*" I licked again, and he parted for me, but I

wasn't done. "Unconditional." One gentle nibble led to another, and Isaac grabbed hold of the back of my head to keep me still.

"Quit it with the teasing and just kiss me," he demanded, tears in his eyes.

So I did.

32

ISAAC

Malachi laid me on my bed and tongued my asshole until I begged for his dick. Still, he refused, dragging out my torture by fingering my hole slow and gentle.

Fucking doctor and his suggestions to take it easy.

I needed my man inside me. Deep and fast. Blowing my goddamn mind.

"Malachi," I groaned as he sank a third finger into my body, stretching and twisting to rub against my prostate. "Jesus...fuck."

Pre-cum oozed from my slit, dripping onto my stomach.

"Getting you good and ready for me, baby—" he leaned in to kiss me "—so I can slide my dick straight into your body without having to work for it.

Want your tight heat sucking me in, swallowing me whole."

"Fuck." I gulped and clutched at the sheets beside me. "Please, Malachi. I'm ready. Just use extra lube and don't stop once you start."

"Needy little bitch."

Fuck, did I love being called that—almost as much as baby.

"*Your* bitch."

Narrowing his gaze, Malachi sat back, taking his fingers with him and leaving me empty and restless. "You mean that?"

Fuck, the vulnerability in his eyes...

"Fuck yes, now hurry," I demanded, breathless. I grabbed hold of my dick, slowly jacking myself, tugging on my balls to calm the fuck down.

He smeared lube down his length, rubbing in time with me. Three strokes and I had enough of the waiting.

"Give me your dick." I lifted my knees, offering him my hole. And of course, his focus went right there.

Moving in, he shook his head, licking his lower lip. "Damn, you are hot as fuck."

"You love me," I sang to him, smirking as he planked over me. "You think I'm sexy—"

Malachi thrust into my body without warning. Balls. Fucking. Deep. "Damn right I do," he groaned between clenched teeth.

He stole my breath, and the stinging stretch of him...fuck the *feel* of him...bare skin—Malachi—without anything between us...

My thoughts fragmented, curses scattering through my brain.

"Fucking hell," I gasped, grabbing his neck and yanking him down. I could have sobbed at how good he felt inside me. "F-fucking need you," my voice broke.

He took my mouth, ignoring the doctor's orders, fucking me into that mattress like he couldn't get enough of me, my body. Every thrust, every moan reminded me blood still roared through my veins, oxygen still filled my lungs.

He'd saved me.

And there wasn't anything I wouldn't give him.

My body took over, moving with him, seeking release. Chasing fulfillment I wouldn't find anywhere outside of him. Nothing separated us, nothing to dim the pleasure of his slickened skin rubbing inside me, over my prostate, jacking my goddamn heartrate and the need to come sky high.

Mine, mine, mine, my mind chanted with every snap of his hips slapping his balls against my body. "Malachi," I whimpered, holding onto him for dear life.

So much damn *fucking* need...

"Come for me, baby." He grabbed my cock and jacked me off in time to his thrusts, sweat dripping down his cheek as he held my gaze. "Shoot your spunk all over your chest. Coat my hand in it."

Fucking hell, his mouth.

He angled his hips, rubbing me just right.

"Oh fuck." I curled upward onto my elbows and watched him fuck into me, panted for oxygen while my dick disappeared in his hand as he rubbed at my glans. "Fucking hell...right there. Don't stop. Fuck, don't st—"

A burst of cum shot up over my chest, and I gasped, reaching out to grab Malachi behind his neck, bringing our mouths together. Heat burst inside my ass, and I swallowed his groan as he thrust into me, both of us shuddering our release until the very last dribble of cum.

I went limp, falling back to the bed, and Malachi came with me, once more smearing a mess between us, our mouths fused as we attempted to suck oxygen between gasping kisses.

He finally relaxed fully, putting his face into my neck, and I let out a sigh that left me boneless. Depleted and completely spent.

"I'm leaving the ministry."

My breath snagged.

Malachi Foley, the man I'd been after for months, had blessed me with so much more than I'd ever hoped for. He was giving up his God, his fucking job...to be with me.

Elation swelled in my chest, and warmth radiated throughout my entire body until my eyes burned with unshed tears. I wrapped my arms around him, smoothing my hands down his back, unsure how he would take my congratulations if I verbalized them.

"I never felt the calling some men do," he continued as I struggled to express my feelings. "I only agreed to go because my mom begged me to while on her deathbed."

Malachi brushed his lips over my neck, sending a shiver over my skin. "I tried to force myself into a box in order to please my parents."

"I know how that feels," I muttered, continuing to caress him, making him aware I understood even though he'd told me his parents had adored him until they'd drawn their final breaths.

He lifted his torso away from mine, his face relaxed, his eyes exhausted. "From the first, I felt a connection to you, like our souls..."

"Recognized each other," I finished for him, rubbing my palm along his scruff.

"It's what drew me to you—your pain, your depression over not feeling 'normal.' Wrong."

"We aren't wrong," I assured him even though I figured he had realized and accepted that.

"We're beautiful." He kissed me, a soft brush of lips that curled my toes. "You're beautiful. Wonderfully made."

I snorted a sarcastic laugh against his mouth

even as my heart flooded over with happiness. "Let's keep one-liners like that in our past, m'kay?"

Malachi chuckled and backed out of my body.

I hissed at the sting, hating the emptiness he left behind even more.

He drew up onto his knees to spread my thighs wide. Wet heat oozed from my sore hole. "My cum looks good on you."

"Mmm?" Another hiss escaped me as he pushed his cum back into my body. "Caveman."

"*Your* man."

Tears once more threatened. "Promise?"

Malachi slid his finger from my ass, caught my gaze and held it, assurance in his eyes. "For eternity, remember?"

So much damn emotion—I didn't know what to do with it. Couldn't vocalize that I felt the same, wanted the same. For eternity.

"Then that means I'm going to your place with you tonight." I went the teasing route, grinning up at him, my heart as light as a feather on a summer breeze. "I'm staying with you—and you're going to let me."

"Damn right." Malachi knelt over me and planted another firm kiss on my lips. "You're adorable, Isaac Van Dusen. Even when you're a brat. Now let's get cleaned up in the shower and head home."

Home.

My heart pinged as a rush of emotion swelled up inside me. One where I would be accepted unconditionally.

That ping in my chest took on a slight ache, and my throat tightened as Malachi walked out of the bedroom. But going there to stay also meant my dreams of Nashville would end before they began.

33

MALACHI

I didn't bother with a suit and tie but decided on slacks and a button-down shirt for my last day of walking into Elkins Bible Church. Dad's old truck rumbled out of my driveway, and I pulled up my best friend's number on my cell to give him an update on what had gone down.

"Hey, Zeke."

"No, *Hello, Ezekiel*?" He chuckled.

I turned out onto the main road, heading toward town. "Not in the teasing mood."

"What's going on?"

No point in shooting the shit. I only had a few miles to travel. "Isaac is in my bed."

"Oh fuck." I could imagine him scrubbing his hand down over his face. "My uncle is going to flip."

"He already did—on Isaac for coming out—but he doesn't know about us yet."

"Us, huh?"

"There's no denying it, no stopping it as far as I'm concerned."

"And what does your conscience tell you?"

"That I've found my other half. The light I've been searching for."

"Shit." Zeke kept silent for a few seconds, and I let him absorb all I'd said.

"I'm heading to the church right now to resign."

"You're giving up God's calling on your life for an eighteen-year-old kid?"

"I never *felt* the call, Zeke," I told him, my voice firm. "Never felt God leading me like the Bible promises. You know I chose that path for my life to make my parents proud, to make up for Brian's death." Even though it *had* been an accident, I quietly reminded myself of what I'd never been able to accept prior to meeting Isaac.

"Is taking a chance with this kid worth eternal damnation?"

I huffed a laugh. "I asked myself the same thing. Countless times. And I've come to the cliche conclusion that being one with him, even for a few moments in time, is worth anything any god might toss my way."

"You've gone so far that you would deny Him?"

I knew the Him Zeke referred to. "I can't believe in a supposed God of love who designs creations with needs and desires that go outside his Word."

"It's because sin entered the world."

"I'm calling bullshit," I stated, sounding like Isaac. "If you had a son, would you allow someone or something to physically alter his makeup? His DNA, the chemicals in his brain, knowing doing so would cause misery? Would you force him to live a lie in order to be on good terms with you? Tell me that isn't fucked up, Zeke. Explain how that isn't cruel."

"My human mind can't fathom it, but I have to believe that God will make himself known—"

"Spare me your canned words, Zeke," I snapped, my chest tightening.

"I guess we'll agree to disagree." His voice held resignation—not judgement.

Elkins Bible Church came into view as I rounded a bend. "You aren't going to shun me for being evil?"

"Nope. You're like my brother, Malachi. We'll just discuss the stuff we do see eye to eye on."

I let out a heavy exhale while turning into the parking lot. My pulse picked up. "Thank you."

"Good luck with my uncle this morning."

Grimacing, I pulled into a parking spot that didn't have the 'Youth Pastor' sign beside where Pastor Bram's car sat. "Going to need it."

I put Dad's truck into park and hung up, steeling myself for the conversation ahead. Pastor Bram wouldn't be as agreeable as Zeke, and it was only out of my feelings for Isaac that I'd decided a face-to-face with his dad was necessary.

After a quick wipe of my palms down my slacks, I stepped from the truck, pebbles crunching beneath my dress shoes. My legs shook a bit while climbing the stairs, the scent of lemons and purity in the church's foyer causing me to gag.

Rather than shying away from the glass doors and the blue carpet leading to the pulpit, I lifted my chin and faced it, sifting through my feelings. Disappointment came first, but not for failing in what I'd promised my parents. The letdown was from the exact things I'd told Zeke about a supposed God of love allowing hurt on His children.

No loving father would do such a thing, and if he did—like Pastor Bram—that man didn't deserve to be called as such.

I'd given God countless hours—days—to reveal himself to me, but he'd stayed silent. He'd left me drowning in darkness when I'd submitted myself wholly, begging for him to guide my steps. I'd found my way with Isaac's help, and it was finally time to live my truth.

Jaw set, I spun away from the place of worship I would never step foot in again and headed back toward the offices.

Mrs. Howard looked up from her computer when I walked into the shared reception area. "Good morning, Pastor Foley."

I forced a smile, glancing to my left. "Is Pastor Bram in?"

"Yes. I'm sure you heard about his son?"

A shot of adrenaline rushed through me, and I faced her. "Hmm?"

She glanced at the pastor's closed office door. "He ran away."

I wondered what else she knew.

"He's eighteen now," I told her as though that made everything okay.

Her lips pursed, and she patted at the gray hairs she'd tucked into a bun. "He's...*gay*," Mrs. Howard whispered. "Pastor Bram unveiled his son's sin to the congregation yesterday during service and asked us to pray for his soul to choose the right path."

The right choice.

I eyed Pastor Bram's door, ready to let him know exactly where I stood. Without a word to the woman I hadn't realized was such a busybody, I strode over and knocked.

"Come in!" Pastor Bram called.

"Pastor Foley." He smiled and motioned me toward the chair across from him. "Welcome back. Welcome back." The supposed joy of the Lord filled his face, and I wondered if he felt any anguish over losing his son.

I sat, lips flatlined, my gut churning.

"How was your time away? Isn't the lake beautiful? It's so relaxing, so easy to feel the Spirit of God when surrounded by his creation."

"I heard about Isaac."

Pastor Bram's joy morphed into visible hatred, scowl lines forming between his eyebrows, his lips downturned. The hardness in his eyes had me shaking my head.

Without a single word from his mouth, I knew *I* had made the right choice.

"I'm resigning," I said before he could spout off any shit about the man I loved. "As of this moment."

"You can't judge me or this church because of Isaac's evil ways," he stated, his eyes widening as he sat back. "That boy chose a reprehensible life over all things holy. I had no influence in his sins!"

"That *boy*," I said, leaning forward and holding his stare with a hard one of my own, "is an adult now and at my apartment. I left him in my bed. Accepted and thoroughly loved. *Sated*," I added for emphasis because fuck him.

Pastor Bram blinked, and I watched the truth of my words dawn on his face. Rage reddened his cheeks, his lips sputtering. "You—you godless heathen!" He slapped his hand on his desk, but I didn't flinch. "You perverted...manipulating... How dare you?" he seethed, showing his teeth. "Sick pedophile. I'll have you thrown in jail!"

I stood, looking down on a man who didn't deserve his son's pain. "Don't waste your time, Bram.

According to Pennsylvania law, he was legal pickings the year before I got here, but even that matter isn't an issue. I love Isaac. Every part of him, every thought, and every emotion he shares. I felt connected to him the second we met in your foyer, and nothing and no one is going to change that fact."

He climbed to his feet too, hands on his desk and tremors rippling down over him. "You're going to burn in hell for corrupting my son."

"If *loving* your son damns me to such a place, I'll stride through those gates willingly." I turned and walked out, thankful as fuck I'd insisted Isaac stay home.

He'd wanted to face his dad as a couple, wanted to support me in what I had to do. I couldn't imagine how his heart ached and what he'd gone through to hide his truth. At least my parents hadn't been dogmatic, legalistic assholes. They probably would have loved me regardless of my sexual orientation if I'd grown the balls to come out publicly. Too bad I hadn't realized that prior to their passing.

But I was done living in the past, wishing I'd done things differently. The path I'd chosen had led me to Elkins.

To Isaac.

"Homosexuality is an abomination to God!" Bram's shriek accompanied my pulling open his office door.

Mrs. Howard hopped up, her face pale, probably

from having heard every word passed between her spiritual leader and one scorned from the flock.

Good fucking riddance.

I strode across the reception area for the other office while Bram spouted off a verse in Romans about committing what is shameful. Recompense—fitting for our ways.

Rather than argue natural law and interpretation with a hypocritical man who didn't know what the word entreatable meant, I set my focus on the future.

I grabbed the lone personal property of mine off my old desk, the last family photo I had from my teenage years. The books I'd studied in seminary sat on a bookshelf against the wall, but I no longer had need or use for those.

"Get out!"

Ignoring the asshole in his office doorway and the quiet, wide-eyed woman watching us, I walked away.

Gladly.

34

ISAAC

I sat curled on Malachi's second-hand couch, journal and pen in hand, but I stared at the stark-white, empty wall across the small space rather than writing. Full of emotions from the best weekend of my life, I struggled to put them into words.

Malachi had left to give his resignation ten minutes earlier, and my good luck wishes were never more meant than in that moment. Knowing what he faced, I cringed, my heartbeat picking up its pace.

Bram Van Dusen would pour damnation down over Malachi's head and attempt to make him repent. I'd warned him of that sure outcome.

He didn't care. Claimed he didn't fear it. We were consenting adults, free to choose our own way, and to hell with what anyone thought.

How far he'd come in the months since we'd

met. Legalistic yet hurting. Dogmatic but broken. Unhappy and struggling.

And now he smiles, his eyes clear. My own smile emerged at the memory of his contented face in my mind.

He'd walked with assurance to his truck while I'd watched from the window, his ass flexing in his slacks and his white button-down stretched over broad shoulders and hiding the tattoos I'd finally gotten to trace with my tongue.

My dad would try to tear him down. Bend him to guilt with words that had been drilled into both my and Malachi's heads since childhood. Having just returned to the "dark side," I wondered over my lover's stubbornness. Would he be easily swayed or manipulated by one of the best into rededicating his life and picking up where he'd left off before giving into the supposed sins of the flesh?

My stomach churned.

"Just stop," I muttered to myself, turning my focus onto the blank page before me. I didn't want to waste one more minute worrying and wondering how his meeting with my dad went—and the possibility of us being over before we'd even really gotten started.

Closing my eyes, I remembered waking in Malachi's arms, memorizing his sleepy blue eyes. Soft skin and hard muscle. How perfectly we fit together when I'd wrapped my legs around his waist.

My dick had no issue figuring out how *he* felt about the whole situation.

I'd been consumed by Malachi...and the inescapable need he satisfied. He drowned me with loving acceptance, and my chest ached from it—for more of it.

Breath exhaling in a rush, I scribbled words illegible to anyone but me, the release of emotion at naming them leaving me as spent as Malachi had earlier that morning. But no tune accompanied my thoughts in black and white chicken scratch. No melody gave meaning and life to mere words.

My cell dinged with an incoming text, and I snatched it off the cushion beside me even though Malachi couldn't have finished with my dad already.

Chris: **Heard you ran away Friday night.**

A heavy, disappointed exhale sagged me back against the couch cushion. **Yeah**, I texted back.

Chris: **Also heard you like dick.**

I pinched my lower lip, not sure how to respond since I couldn't see his face or hear his tone. "Fuck." After another minute of inner debate, I started to type an affirmative response, but the cell rang before I hit send.

"Shit." Swallowing, I swiped to answer Chris's call. "Hey."

"The fuck, man?"

"What?" I asked, my entire body tensing over the anger in his voice.

"You're fucking gay? After all that shit about girls, tits, and ass. Seriously?"

I'd decided to live my truth, so I owned it, knowing I'd already lost his friendship. "Yeah. I like dick. You should try it sometime. It's fucking fantastic—especially shoved down your throat."

"You sick fuck!" Chris cursed, painting a clear picture of what he thought about homosexuality—exactly as I'd expected. "You're a liar of the worst sort."

"*You're* the liar, asshole," I shot back, my brow furrowed and my free hand fisting. "Pretending to be a good Christian boy. You get one girl pregnant, turn your back on her, then try to corrupt Sara all while putting on another face for your parents and the church."

"You piece of sh—"

"Don't go pointing out my *sins* and ignore the fucking plank in your own eye, Chris." I hit end and went straight into his info, blocking his number with shaking fingers.

Fuck him, and fuck everyone who thought like him.

Swallowing hard, I closed my eyes and tipped my head back, waiting for the adrenaline to finish with my body. I counted backwards from ten in a rhythm matching my heart's dancing cadence. I breathed, pausing for a beat. Steadying thumps took back up in my head...

A rhythm rose, the rolling emotions inside me coming to life in a whispered note...another. Slow as a rising sun, complex and yet pulling in the familiar that those with eyes—or in my case—*ears* could relate to.

Innovative and personal, just like all the other music I'd written.

I didn't doubt I belonged in Nashville.

Throat tight, I picked up my guitar and let my gift lead me—as I would have to do regardless of Malachi's time with my dad. But would my heart be willing to go if it came down to choosing between him and my dream?

I closed my eyes and played, pouring my emotion into the words I knew Malachi would understand without me having to explain.

35

MALACHI

I heard Isaac's voice and guitar from where I stood outside my apartment door—and my hand froze from sliding the key into the lock. A haunting melody, simple chord progressions, but...something *more*.

Out of the ordinary and in some way familiar enough that the notes drew me in.

As quietly as possible, I let myself into my apartment, my focus falling to the back of his dark head bent over his guitar. His raspy voice held a uniqueness I hadn't heard from modern music. Pure, raw emotion. And the way his graceful fingers plucked over the strings? Isaac took listeners along for a ride.

Major labels in the music industry didn't like taking risks, but they no longer mattered as much as they used to—and what Isaac had couldn't be ignored. Advancing technology allowed for production and distribution outside the norm, and my heart raced over the idea of helping him achieve his dreams.

It wouldn't require Nashville.

We could do it together—wherever the fuck we made our bed.

Our bed.

Throat tight, I listened to his clear artistic voice and allowed his emotions to take me along where he went.

Consuming.

Inescapable.

Drowning and aching.

Love...

I lived the words pouring from his lips for another moment, and I stood speechless as the notes faded into silence. He hadn't said it out loud—neither had I, but the sense of more than lust between us had been put to music.

"I know you're there," Isaac said, finally angling to look at me over the back of the couch.

Of course he did, same as I always knew when he entered a room.

Overwhelmed with the hurt in his eyes and my love for him, I strode across the apartment, grasped his face in my hands, and kissed him. Hard and hungry. Wanting to spill the tears building in my eyes.

"What was that?" I whispered against his cinnamon-flavored mouth, both of us breathless.

"My mind's ramblings from the weekend." His eyes held a sheen, same as mine. "My...emotions that I'm not good at communicating."

"I'd say you did a damn good job of telling me how you feel about me," I said, breathless from finally knowing his heart.

"Yeah?"

I grinned and gave him another quick kiss, my stomach fluttering. "Yeah." I rounded the couch and sat beside him since he still held his guitar like a shield. "Want to talk about it?"

"How'd it go with my dad?"

Guess not.

Accepting his boundaries over the ramblings he'd put to music didn't come easily. I swallowed against the disappointment of not exploring what ebbed and flowed between us like a rolling wave, the exact harmony I'd heard in my head as he sang. "Not good."

Isaac snorted, turning away to set his guitar in the case on the coffee table. "Not surprised."

I sat back, giving him space as I shared the shit that had gone down at Elkins Bible Church. Refusing to hide anything from Isaac, I disclosed all his dad had said, even the "Get out" he'd commanded, same as he'd done to his son the Friday before.

"I'm sorry you had to go through that," Isaac muttered, his brow furrowed while he picked at imaginary lint on his gym shorts.

"I'm sorry you had to put up with that kind of legalism your whole life," I told him the God's honest truth.

Fuck that—my truth.

He tried for a grin and looked up at me. "I want to get out of here, Malachi," Isaac said, his voice quiet. "Away from the church's hatred and the back-woods bigots. This society's lies and judgements. Chris and Tyler. I need to experience a different life. I'm only eighteen. I've got plenty of time to make up for all I missed out on."

Yeah, he did. But how long until he realized there was more than Malachi Foley available for the taking? We fit perfectly together in our current head-space and situation, but what about down the road when he changed his present and made a name for himself? When he got a taste of the world outside the sticks of Pennsylvania?

When adoring fans threw themselves at him, offering whatever he desired? Their hearts. Their bodies. Their souls.

He already owned all three of mine, but would he crave more than I could ever give him—even if it was my everything?

I opened my mouth to tell him my feelings but closed it at the thought that I'd be pushing him into choices *I* wanted for him. He'd probably see it as nothing more than an attempt to handle him since that's all he'd ever known from his dad.

Fuck, relationships were hard.

"So now what?" Isaac asked when I didn't respond.

I held out my hand, my chest aching. I needed to feel him against me, his heart beating in time with mine. "We live happily ever after?" I asked with a joking tone so it wouldn't be taken as manipulation.

Isaac crawled onto my lap, his smile unsure enough that the pain in my chest remained.

"We relax for a few weeks," I suggested something other than a fairytale, putting aside my own desires and focusing on the present. "We get to know one another better and decide what we're going to do, where we're going to go."

Rather than argue the togetherness of my suggestion, Isaac released a heavy sigh and snuggled into me. He melted in my arms exactly how I needed in that moment, letting me know I was his home, I was his comfort.

I'm his knight in shining armor—for now.

Focusing on the positives, I held him close. Kissed his hair that smelled like my shampoo and released a heavy sigh of my own.

We would be okay.

We had to be.

36

ISAAC

We went with the flow, just like Malachi suggested. Singing and writing music together when we weren't job searching. Neither of us wanted to up and move without having direction. And seeing as how I refused to mow lawns in a neighborhood close to my parents, we searched outside of Elkins—in the opposite direction of the church.

All the while, we uploaded our recordings to social media sites that supported music.

Malachi had a digital audio workstation on his computer from years earlier. Add in a monitor and microphone he'd had tucked in a box in the back of his closet and we made our own "recording studio" right there in our living room.

Writing and creating music—gorgeous harmonies—was our passion, one we excelled at.

Together.

My dreams for Nashville morphed into more than fame and fortune with every day I spent with Malachi hunched over our guitars and my journals. I still planned to go, but I wanted him there with me. Creating music together. As partners—and not just in business.

But I couldn't find the words to tell him, and guilt rose whenever he hinted at his feelings toward me and I went the joke route to lighten the seriousness between us.

We uploaded my songs to every platform we could, and within two weeks, without even trying, I had a fanbase of a couple hundred strangers. Those listeners made it easy to find coffee houses and bars with open mic nights close by, slowly widening our reach.

I walked on air, hand in hand with Malachi, heading into the grocery store. We'd had our first gig in Scranton the night before, a big city compared to Elkins, and the reception we got, the bar's patrons crowding around us once we finished...

They hadn't even cared that we'd kissed right there on stage after the final song.

Fucking perfection. We landed three more gigs because of that performance and were well on our way to growing a solid foundation for our dreams.

My face hurt from smiling—but the grin died

when Chris and Tyler exited the grocery store in front of us.

Chris glanced up after pulling his keys from his back pocket, and our gazes connected. His focus went from me to Malachi, to our clasped hands, and back to my face. "Fucking faggots," he muttered loud enough to reach our ears over the distance separating us.

Tyler's gaze jerked toward us, his face paling as his footsteps stuttered. Regret filled his face, tugging his lips downward.

A few other people nearby glanced at us, but I lifted my chin and held on tighter to Malachi's hand. Let the fuckers judge. Let them talk.

Chris turned away, but Tyler hesitated. He opened his mouth. Closed it. And hurried after his friend.

The second we walked into the store's air-conditioned vastness, my shoulders sagged, but the twisting in my stomach over losing my only friends remained.

"You okay?" Malachi murmured, pulling a grocery cart from the line of them just inside the automatic doors.

"Yeah." I'd told him about my conversation with Chris weeks earlier, and he'd been ready to go beat the shithead into the ground. We'd agreed he wasn't worth our time, but I'd felt Malachi's tension at Chris's name calling.

"I want to wrap you up and take you home. Fucking hate that you have to deal with that shit," Malachi muttered.

"I'm not going to let some asshole hurt me enough to be too scared to go into public or stand on stage beside you. Are *you* okay?" I asked, hating the furrow between his eyebrows.

Lips tight, he nodded.

"I'm proud of you," I whispered, leaning against his side, blowing hot air over his ear.

He shivered and turned down the dairy aisle. "Proud of you too. I love how you're unapologetically you."

Love...a word we'd used in passing but not directly. I felt it though, and I knew he did too. For as much as we pushed to get emotions into my journals in prep for music, we should have been whispering that sentiment every other minute of the day.

However, soft touches and the brush of lips not intending to lead to sex but to affirm our appreciation of one another—I'd rather have those things my heart craved than my ears filled with mere words. Hell only knew I'd heard enough of the preaching about love without the practice from Dad.

Feeling lighter, I grabbed the week's flyer from the cart he pushed and flipped to the back for the frozen food sales. "Lasagna!" I said with a grin. "Your favorite brand too."

"Sweet."

Neither of us could cook much, but we put his portable grill to good use. I wished I'd paid more attention to what Mom did in the kitchen and learned from her so I could provide in the ways I knew a woman never would for me.

When it came to "women's work" as Dad had called it, Malachi and I were screwed. But we made do. Shared chores. Attempted to create decent enough tasting food together.

But frozen lasagna?

Delicious and as close to a home cooked meal I feared we'd ever get until we made it big and could afford a full-time chef.

We ambled through the store, shoulders and hips brushing on occasion, every touch intentional as we shopped, causing Chris's bigotry to fade from my mind.

Thinking on the upcoming shows we would perform together, my happiness returned. I even grabbed Malachi's backside when we entered an aisle and found ourselves alone. I couldn't get enough of the man. His hands and mouth on me, the ass he let me own whenever I wanted. Sharing cum and secrets. Cuddles—

Mom appeared at the aisle's end, her cart's forward momentum jerking to a stop as our gazes clashed. "Isaac," she whispered, ragged, her entire body seeming to sag where she stood.

Dad didn't appear beside her, but he never did

the wife's responsibilities. I didn't need to fear facing him in that moment.

"Mom." I stepped past Malachi and went to her, noting she'd lost weight when she couldn't afford to.

Tears filled her eyes and slid down her cheeks, and my throat tightened.

Rather than turning away like her husband would have demanded, she came to me. Hugged me. Squeezed me, letting out a quiet sob.

Mom. Smelling like fresh baked bread and flowers. Soft and comforting.

I choked on a sob of my own, knowing our moment couldn't last, so I soaked that shit up. Breathed in her subtle perfume, the dark hair escaping her bun brushing against my nose.

Her arms told me more than any words possibly could. She loved me. No matter what. And when she stepped away, her eyes said the same. "You're still here."

"For now."

She glanced at Malachi behind me, offering him a smile that didn't reek of hypocrisy. "Are you happy?" Mom asked, her focus returning to me.

"More than I thought possible."

Her smile wobbled as more wetness rose to coat her eyes. "Please keep in touch with me," she whispered as though afraid Dad would hear. "Let me know you're alright."

"Maybe we could meet for breakfast someday soon."

She hesitated to answer.

"Or not. I don't want to get you in trouble." I forced a smile and leaned in to kiss her soft cheek. "I'll text. Promise."

Nodding and hands shaking, she retrieved her cart, and we passed in the aisle, going our separate ways, both of us swiping tears from the corners of our eyes.

Malachi laced his fingers through mine, but he didn't speak. I took the time he offered to settle in my heart that Mom and I had closure.

And while I wished she would leave my asshole of a dad and find a better life, a better partner, I knew she never would. For her, love was blind, and I couldn't fault her for that.

I stared at the blond beside me who needed a haircut, but that scruff he'd been lazy about could stay. He looked sexy as fuck, unkempt with his wrinkled T-shirt, and perfect.

Mine.

Even if we never made it to the big time, I knew I would be content.

We unloaded the groceries onto the belt, the magazine rack catching my eye and making me question what I'd thought true seconds earlier.

Rolling Stone's latest cover showed the young girl who'd created a splash in the music industry earlier in the year. At mere fifteen, she'd signed with Columbia thanks to her music videos that had gone viral on social media.

She wasn't exactly unique in voice or song writing, but her reach, her fans, promised the record execs big money. They'd been quick to gobble her up and blast her face and music across the world, reaching listeners her lyrics resonated with.

I craved what she'd accomplished. My heart ached for it.

I wanted to find and connect with people who felt and thought the same as I did. I wanted to stand on stage and take them on an emotional journey. I wanted them to accept and appreciate the gift I knew I had.

Would having a couple hundred followers be enough?

I glanced at Malachi talking to the cashier, his smile easy. Gorgeous. My heart ached even as my dick twitched.

It will *be enough,* I promised myself, even though a seed of doubt remained long after we loaded up his truck with groceries and drove home.

37
____

MALACHI

For a week, Isaac seemed broody, escaping back inside himself. While not closed off to me physically, I could feel the distance separating our hearts and minds.

And both of mine sat uneasy.

Discontented in some way, he kept quiet. Knowing his past of utilizing his journal more than his mouth, I let him do what he needed to figure out whatever was bothering him.

But I moved forward with my plans.

I headed out for a few errands, leaving him behind on the couch with his guitar as he struggled with the song we'd been working on together for a few days and wanted to reveal at the gig we had the following night.

Once around the corner from the apartment, I

pulled off the road and searched for a number I feared calling.

She answered after three rings.

"Jennifer," I greeted, ready for her to disconnect without a word.

"Malachi! How are you doing? Are you okay?"

I wondered what she'd heard through the grapevine.

"I'm really well."

"I'm so glad to hear it." Her bubbly voice assured me she didn't lie.

"What else have people been saying?" Might as well get the shit out on the table before she asked why I'd called. It would doubtless be a deciding factor.

"That you stole Isaac away and you're living in sin."

Well, she didn't pull any punches. I couldn't help my chuckle. "It's more like Isaac came on to me, I couldn't deny him, and now we're attempting a happily ever after."

She actually laughed lightly, relaxing me back into my driver's seat. "We miss you—the teens miss you."

"They don't think I'm going to burn in hell?"

"They haven't been taught anything different, but your teachings the past couple of months have instilled grace and mercy. A new concept, but more easily accepted by those younger in the church."

"And you?"

"It's not my place to judge, Malachi. You'll stand or fall before God alone when the day comes. But I know your heart and the love you've shown these kids. It's the love of a true Christian whether you consider yourself one anymore or not."

My throat grew tight. "If only more believers thought like you did."

"Yeah, it's a shame how much hatred and hypocrisy are out there these days."

I considered her cousin, our past—the reason for my call.

"I have a favor to ask," I forced myself to say, all for Isaac.

"Anything."

"Is there any chance I could get your cousin's number? The one who lives in Nashville?"

"About that..."

My insides clenched tight.

"...he's left the Christian music industry."

"Should I offer congratulations?"

Jennifer laughed again. "He said he's moving onward and upward in the world. He works for Cadence Records now."

Cadence—the biggest label when it came to unique music. And two of their musicians had topped the charts for three weeks and counting.

Pure luck or an even greater letdown?

"Do you want me to get in touch with him to tell

him who you are, that you're going to be calling?" she asked.

I cleared my throat, wanting to keep his and my past exactly that—in our past. "I'd rather just get his number than use you more than I already feel I am."

"It's not using, Malachi. I'd be happy to give you his number."

I obtained Elliot James's cell number after a few more minutes of learning about his life-changing decision and dialed him up, my heart in my throat. Adrenaline running. For years, I'd despised the man for what he'd done, how he'd taken advantage of me and others, but my feelings for Isaac trumped my resentment and need for revenge. Cliché to think that love could conquer all, but for me, it did. Nothing was more important than Isaac.

I'd given up a promise to my mom for him, so what was facing another part of my past if it would make his dreams come true?

Elliot James didn't answer, but I left a detailed message so he would know exactly who I was and why I called. While I'd have preferred cursing him out and punching his teeth in, swallowing my pride meant a chance for Isaac.

And there wasn't anything I wouldn't do for my lover, my light.

Even if it meant I got left behind.

38

ISAAC

We landed "real" jobs, and Malachi and I slaved together side by side along with a guy named Manuel at Johnson's Orchard. Five days a week, eight-to-ten-hour days depending on what needed done. Apple season had started, the busiest time of the year for them.

And at night, we pursued our shared passion—without the goofy Mexican guy who didn't care that we were as gay as unicorns and proud of it.

Singing together, my writing, and Malachi's recording and producing was what drove us through the long hours until weekend gigs. We shared our music on social media, his excitement over follower numbers keeping me happy, content at our progress in chasing the dream while sweating our asses off during the daytime hours.

Our music followed us through the orchard, and

we got caught up singing a cappella, silly ditties about rotten apples and dripping sweat. Late summer's sun gifted us with farmer's tans while we dreamed about being on a bigger stage together.

Shirtless and sweaty, we lounged with Manuel beneath an oak tree at the orchard's edge for lunch on Friday, same as we always did for break.

"Malachi said you got a couple new TikTok followers overnight," Manuel said, crunching into an apple he'd taken from the last bin we'd filled.

"A couple?" I laughed. "Over a thousand. All because of a new video we'd posted of the two of us singing yesterday."

"I saw it," Manuel said, chewing with his mouthful. "Went fucking viral in less than twenty-four hours."

Malachi and I shared a grin.

"You two are fucking awesome," Manuel said. "Like seriously. Damn good music, cool as shit voices, and the way you look at each other when singing... Yeah. Never heard anything like you two. When you make it to the big time, I'm going to cash in on that, you know. I was your first and biggest fan."

"Too bad you can't sing worth a shit," I tossed back, feeling lighter than I had in weeks. "We'd pull you in for backup."

"My back aint getting anywhere near your horny asses," he said, tossing the core at my head.

Malachi's cell rang, cutting into our laughter. He grabbed the phone from his pocket.

"Hold on a sec," he said, still grinning. His smile faded as he looked at the screen. "Be right back." He hopped up while answering with a "Hello," his stride taking him out of earshot.

I glanced at Manuel, and he shrugged. My gaze returned to Malachi's tensed shoulders and wide stance as he stood a few dozen feet away.

"Whoever it was, he didn't look too happy about the call," Manuel said, eyeing me.

"Yeah." I blew out a breath and crumpled up the baggie my sandwich had been inside. "Don't know who the fuck it could be though."

Manuel and I sat silent, but none of Malachi's murmurs could be made out from the distance he'd put between us.

Sitting forward in the grass, knees drawn up, I bit into the apple I'd taken from the bin. Sweet juice burst on my tongue, but my stomach soured over the worries in my mind going rampant.

Malachi shoved the cell back in his pocket. Hands on his hips, he tipped his head back as though in prayer.

My heart stumbled as thoughts scrambled in my head. He had no other family, so it wouldn't be bad news like a death or something. Had Zeke called? I hardly knew my older cousin, but Malachi told me he'd been struggling lately with some personal shit he wouldn't talk about.

Maybe he'd finally caved and unloaded to Malachi, asking for prayer?

Shit.

I gulped a few swallows of tepid water from my jug, my gaze glued to him.

"Any idea what's going on?" Manuel murmured, and I shook my head.

"No fucking clue." My voice came out tight. Strained. Same as my temples.

"Doesn't seem good."

"Thanks, Mr. Positive."

"Sorry. Just sayin'."

"Yeah, I know. Fuck, Malachi, turn around and tell me—"

He turned.

And his smile kicked me in the gut, making me choke down what I'd been saying. I'd never seen him so...thrilled before. Even when balls deep in my ass, spent, and shivering, he didn't appear so damn content.

"Guess it *was* good," Manuel said, but I couldn't tear my gaze off Malachi.

Quick strides brought him back, and he yanked me up off the ground and into his arms.

The half-eaten apple in my hand fell to the ground, forgotten.

Manual made fake gagging noises whenever our

PDA got out of control, but I ignored him, gladly taking all Malachi gave, every lash of his tongue causing my heart to race and blood to heat.

"Fuck, you taste damn delicious," he groaned against my mouth before diving in for more. "Like a damn apple pie."

"What was that for?" I asked, breathless when he finally put me back on my feet.

His blue eyes glowed, his grin so damn contagious that my chest fluttered. "I called Elliot James a few weeks ago," he said, the name kicking into my memory within a heartbeat.

"Jennifer's cousin."

"He works for Cadence Records now," Malachi said with a nod. "He checked out your work on social media—and he wants you to come to Nashville."

Holy shit balls.

I laughed. "You're full of it."

"Nope. I gave him your number, and he's going to give you a buzz later tonight to go over some details."

"Holy *fuck*!"

"Right?" Light still filled his face, but the glow inside me dimmed slightly.

My social media, Malachi had said. Elliot wanted *me* to go to Nashville.

"He knows we're a duo, right?" I asked.

His smile faded, and he grasped me behind my

neck, holding me close. Eyes on my lips, he let out a heavy exhale.

"Elliot James and I have a past, Isaac."

Nashville.

Malachi's time of rebellion and hitting rock bottom.

He'd told me a record executive had taken advantage of him, lied to him.

Holy shit. Fucking hell...

"Elliot was the one who hurt you," I whispered the thought as it came. He'd actually called the fucker who'd used him...for me. Chest tight as fuck and eyes stinging, I swallowed hard.

He nodded, lifting his focus to my eyes. Trouble filled his, and I grabbed hold of his waist as I felt his instinct to pull away from me. "Why would you trust him with what we've built?"

"Because he came out three months ago, Jennifer told me. He left Christian radio—and I'm willing to take advantage of his connections. I'll do whatever I have to do to make this happen for you."

I chewed on the inside of my lip, studying his face, seeing the decision he'd already come to clearly in his eyes.

Malachi would face bullshit from his past and dig up emotions best left to rest in order to see me succeed.

Fuck. Could I love the man any more than I already did?

I laid my hand on his chest, feeling the steady thump that soothed me whenever I couldn't sleep, the connection between us stronger than ever. "You're going with me." I wouldn't take no for an answer.

He caressed behind my ear with his thumb, the rest of his fingers clasping tight to my neck. "I don't think Elliot and I will ever be the greatest of friends."

"I figured."

"But if you want me beside you through this, I'll face down the fucking devil himself to see you through."

"Good thing you boys don't believe in that red dude with horns," Manual said from behind us, reminding us we weren't alone.

I chuckled. "Yeah," I agreed. "So. *We* are headed to Nashville."

The light returned to Malachi's face, the beauty of his stare filling me up. "If that's what you want."

"I do."

He kissed me, and Manuel let out a whoop.

A few hours later, I pushed Malachi down onto our bed, uncaring that his skin would taste salty as fuck. He shoved off his jeans, and I did the same, desperate to get on him. Show him how much he meant to me, how much I needed him since I still couldn't find the fucking words.

I went for his already hard dick, but he grabbed

hold of my head. "You don't want to suck sweaty dick, baby, trust me. Just lube me up and ride me."

I grabbed the bottle off our bedstand, my hands shaking, so much damn joy bubbling inside me that I almost laughed. Flipping the cap, I glanced up to find Malachi's smile gone, hesitation in his eyes when he'd been full of lust seconds earlier.

"What's wrong?" I asked, pausing in my drive to get him slickened up and inside my body.

"I'm afraid the fame will tear us apart—and I don't say that to manipulate you in any way," he hastened to add. "I just never want to be anything but honest with you."

My breath left in a rush.

"No other man, no other dick will ever compare," I said, trying for the most assured tone and look I could offer while dribbling lube over his length that hadn't flagged one bit.

"You've never had another dick." He groaned, watching as I jacked him.

"I don't *want* another dick," I told him the God's honest truth, climbing to hover over him, too impatient to prep. "Give me yours."

"Gladly—fucking always." Malachi grabbed hold of my hips and pulled me down, lifting his torso to take my mouth. I was claimed with one slow, sinking stroke. Filled. Never surer of my thoughts toward him and the emotions I desperately needed to spill from my lips.

Seconds later, I lay on my back, holding Malachi's stare as he glided in and out of my body, every rub over my prostate leaking precum from my slit onto my belly. Our gazes held, nothing between us. Like he knew my mind, he thrust and ground against me exactly how I craved.

Fuck, I could totally lose myself in his light eyes—clear down to his beautiful soul. He never hid his thoughts, his feelings—

"You're so fucking sexy," he said, his tone rasped, sending readiness tingling through my balls.

"I love you." The words came easier than expected, from an abundance of delicious perfection, complete happiness dwelling inside my chest.

His eyes welled, and he sank in deep, lowering his heat over my torso with a heavy sigh as though he'd been waiting to hear those words from me. "I feel like I've loved you forever."

A brush of lips turned into hungry kisses. Caressing hands grasped, and fingertips dug into muscle.

And he whisper-groaned my name while we came together.

As one.

39

MALACHI

ONE YEAR LATER...

Isaac lay on the bed completely bare, his pale, beautiful skin still covered with water droplets and his cell phone held to his ear.

I stood in the bathroom doorway, drying off my hair from the shower we'd just taken. A celebratory one after a ball-draining fuck against the hotel's wall an hour earlier.

"Yeah," he said into his cell, his hazel eyes darkening as his gaze slid down over my body. "He's doing well, Mom. We both are."

How far I'd come in a year. From denying myself, stumbling through the darkness, and pleading for fulfillment and light...to finding the home I'd craved.

I tossed aside my towel and climbed onto the bed beside the young man who gave my life purpose, propping up on an elbow and entwining one of my legs between his. He shifted onto his side, bringing us face to face.

My beautiful lover with his still-smooth cheeks, pouty lips...and the small heart he'd gotten tattooed on his left pec. Our initials rested inside, scripted from music notes. Mine lay over my right pec above the piercings he'd suggested I get.

The ones I begged him to tongue whenever he put his mouth on me.

"I'll call you as soon as we're done," he told his mom, smiling at me, the adoration in his eyes making me feel like the richest man on the face of the earth.

Tomorrow it begins...

Our first tour would kick off in Nashville the following evening. We'd been dubbed the cliche dynamic duo, and radio stations and the charts loved us.

From day one, Isaac had declared us a team. Partners no matter what.

Elliot James and I never once spoke of our past, and while I still wanted to smash in his nose on occasion when he got too bossy, I kept my cool. Just told him to let us have things the way we wanted or we'd take our talent elsewhere.

And that talent had landed us the record deal with Cadence I hoped for. Going on tour come morning.

"He's my everything, Mom."

Fuck. I swallowed hard, and our gazes locked, my heart beating heavy in my chest.

"I'm so happy for you, son," I could hear her voice through the cell. "Truly."

"Malachi's the best decision I ever made."

Her murmurs of love came through, and I thanked fate that at least one of his parents had decided to accept and keep in touch with their son.

"Love you too, Mom."

I brushed my thumb over Isaac's lower lip as he hung up and tossed his cell to the side. He snuggled in against me, all damp, warm skin and fresh cinnamon-laced breath.

"Everything okay?" I asked.

"Yeah." He kissed me lightly and relaxed, letting out a sigh. "Dad asks about me on occasion, and he's finally stopped ranting his fire and brimstone bullshit."

One thing I definitely didn't miss about our past—too long sermons about a God of love who didn't deserve worship. Accepting my truth hadn't come easily, and I'd dragged my feet for months, but Isaac had proven too much a temptation, too much of a force of nature.

Looking back, I realized my heart, my soul, hadn't stood a chance of denying us.

"Beautifully Us" was the first track of our album, one already hailed legendary by the LGBT community. Our people. Our family. People who loved without hypocrisy.

"Think he'll ever accept the life you've chosen?" I asked, smoothing his damp hair off his forehead.

"Nope—and I don't care if he doesn't."

Isaac and I had both come far in letting out the thoughts and feelings we'd kept bottled up for years. It took time for personal growth of that magnitude, but having a partner willing to put in the effort, the desire to help the other become a better person, made it easier.

"She said she's proud of me, and that's enough. I don't need Dad's approval when I have hers and yours."

We kissed and snuggled for a few minutes, simply being present and enjoying the quiet before the unknown storm of the next day to come.

Bright lights.

Screaming fans.

Singing for the first time in front of a crowd bigger than a few thousand. Isaac owned the stage whenever he stood there with his guitar, face glowing. Voice sure and steady while singing into the mic and drawing in listeners in for the ride of their life.

But he always turned toward me when I joined in the chorus, strumming along on my own guitar in time with his. Our voices weaving without effort, creating beauty like I'd never known. Both of us side by side, same as Johnny and his June.

And our fans loved us. Together, publicly claimed partners, hopelessly in love.

"Ready to make our dreams come true?" Isaac asked, rubbing his palm over my scruffy cheek.

I leaned into his touch but focused on his eyes. "You can start by making *my* most important one come true."

"What's that?"

Threading his fingers through mine, I lifted his hand to my lips, kissing his ring finger. It was time to share the last things in my heart and mind I'd withheld from him. And not out of fear or manipulation to keep him close but because I loved him. Everything about him.

"Marry me," I whispered. "Take my last name. Be mine forever."

Smirking, he turned our hands and bit the back of my thumb. "I already am, but if your insecure ass needs a paper..."

With a growl, I rolled Isaac onto his back, pinning him in place. "Brat."

His gaze narrowed as his lips quirked into a full-on smile. "You love it."

"I love *you*," I told him, grinding my swelling dick against his.

"Show me how much."

"Gladly." I took his mouth and gave him what he wanted, and when the next night came, we walked hand in hand onto stage.

To screaming fans and blinding spotlights.

Isaac's flushed face, the energy radiating off him filled me up with the kind of peace I'd searched for my entire life. I'd found heaven on earth in the arms of a forbidden love.

And I would worship him until we breathed our last.

THE END

———

ABOUT THE AUTHOR

Lynn Burke is an international bestselling and award-winning author. A stay-at-home mom, she's a lover of coffee and vino, and with three spawn and two fur babies underfoot, noise levels dictate the daily switch-over time. In her few quiet 'me' moments, she can be found hunched over her Mac, trying to type as fast as her muse spews hot stories.

You can find more about Lynn at her website: www.authorlynnburke.com

ALSO BY LYNN BURKE

Abel's Obsession

Divulging Secrets

Healing Storms

In Between

Reluctant Lumberjack

Resisting his Mate

The Playboy Bachelor

Billion Dollar Love Anthology

Blood Born Series

Bonds of Worship Series

Dark Leopards MC

Darkest Desires Series

Devil's Outlaws MC

Elite Escort Series

Fallen Gliders MC

Forbidden Obsession Duet

Found by Fate Series

Midnight Sun Series

Missing Link Series

Risso Family Series

Sandy Ridge Series

Sinful Nature Series

Vicious Vipers MC